Breaking Point

By Dylan Rogers

Table of Contents

Chapter 1: The Fight

As a pessimistic 18-year-old boy living in the most embarrassing era in the history of the modern world, Alex Underwood saw himself as the lone cultural genius living in a world filled with an alarming amount of stupid people. He gave a middle finger to the modern world, and shortly after the death of his father, his family as well. Alex's mother tried her best to keep things in order around the house and in their family, but that was no easy task, given the son she was dealing with, along with an emotionally scarred 14-year-old daughter.

One day his mother came home from work to find that Alex still hadn't done any chore she had asked of him. Instead, Alex sat up in his room without a care in the world, talking to his friend Andrew on the phone.

"What about Tiffany, she's pretty cute," Alex said into the phone while lying on the bed, the phone on speaker with his hands occupied by a video game controller, ignoring the fact that he has a girlfriend of his own. "I bet she'd go with you. I know I'd *go* with her, if you know what I mean."

"I don't know man, I don't think she's that into me, and she would never say yes. I probably just won't go. I haven't even found a nice suit."

"God, you're such a chick, just wear jeans and a nice shirt like you dress your body pillow every night. It's homecoming, not prom, it's not a big deal."

"Oh yeah you're quite the comedian," Andrew joked through the phone. "Hey, you want to kick the ball around up at the high school? I have some time to kill before I meet my mom for lunch."

"Yeah sure, let me get my stuff together and I'll meet you there."

Before Alex could end the call his mother exploded into his room with a frustrated look masking her usually content personality.

"Hang up the damn phone, Alex," she said, burying her steaming red face into her hands. "Why can't you do just *one* thing I ask of you? Your sister and I do everything around the house while you just sit up here eating junk, playing video games, and jerking off all day."

"What the hell is your problem? Get out of my room!" Alex stood up and grabbed his jacket and keys.

"Damn it Alex what happened? Before your father died you were one of the happiest boys ever, now you act like the world owes you for God knows what reason. When he died I told you I needed you to step up and help me and you just shut down, why? What goes on in your mind to make you act this way?"

"How about you being a complete bitch?" Alex snapped back. "All I want is for you to just get off my back for 10 seconds, but no, you always find a reason to come yell at me. 'Oh Alex do your homework', 'oh Alex take care of your sister', if you would just shut the fuck up for *once* maybe I would give a shit about you."

"Why can't you just be like your sister, Alex," his mother muttered, almost inaudible before breaking into tears.

"Yeah, and why can't you just be like your husband, huh, dead?" Alex stormed past his mother and out of the house, his mother left in his room, now on her knees. No more crying, no more yelling, just absolute shock and heartbreak. Alex's sister ran into the room and hugged her mother.

"I'm so sorry Mom, you know he didn't mean it," she said, almost in tears herself.

"I know; that's not what hurts. What hurts is that he actually thinks he does mean it."

Up at the high school, Alex and Andrew were doing a little one-on-one scrimmage for about a half hour in preparation for the next season. They were the best soccer players in school, and this was their last year.

"Hey Alex," Andrew said kicking the ball to him, "why you look so upset?"

"My freaking mom got on me again." Alex kicked the ball back abnormally uninspired. "What do you do when your mom yells at you?"

"Oh, well uh, my mom doesn't really yell at me. We have a good relationship."

"Oh well aren't you a peach. How long do we have before you have to meet your mom for lunch?"

"I'm supposed to be there at noon I think." Andrew looked at his phone. "Oh damn, I lost track of time, it's ten to noon, I got to go." Andrew grabbed his ball and keys.

"All right man that's cool; maybe meet up again a little later? We need to practice our long pass."

"Yeah sorry, I wish I could, but I have homework and dinner and all that, so I probably won't have time. Maybe tomorrow, I'll let you know."

"Uh yeah sure, sounds good. Have fun at lunch," Alex said sarcastically. He could never tell Andrew, but hearing him talk about how great his life had been was nauseating to say the least. On the way back to his car, Alex called his girlfriend, Hailey.

"Hey babe, what's up?" Hailey answered enthusiastically.

"Come with me, let's go explore," Alex said. That was something he had said at the beginning of nearly every conversation with her for years. It was their own inside joke. "Do you want to meet me at Wal-Mart? I just got done practicing and need to get some new shoes and something to eat."

"Yeah totally, I'll meet you up in the usual spot in the parking lot!"

"See you there." Alex hung up the phone with a smile on his face. At least he had one good thing in his life. Hailey had been in France with her family for the last month, so he couldn't see her. He hadn't seen her all summer, which made this even sweeter.

Alex figured it best if he didn't go home right away. He didn't want to face his mom again, and wasn't ready to apologize, even though he was really bothered about what he had said.

He pulled into the parking lot and saw Hailey standing next to her 1997 Honda Civic. The car was a total junker, but hey, it was a car.

"Hey babe." Alex got out and kissed her on the cheek and they started to walk inside, "How was France?"

"Oh it was amazing! The food was awful for the most part, but the museums were exquisite."

"Awesome, I wish I could've been there. Do you need anything while we are here?"

"I don't think so, no. What kind of shoes are you thinking of getting?"

"I need some running shoes; my old ones were getting all torn up. Never buy any Asics shoes, they reel you in with their flashy colors and high prices making it out to be a great shoe, but they all suck. I'm going to buy some New Balance or Nike shoes. They have the best durability rating by far."

"You and your shoes," Hailey said laughing. Alex thrives on having a high level of knowledge on things that didn't matter, like shoes and car tires. The only person who understood and shared that thirst for irrelevant knowledge was Andrew, which explained their inseparable friendship. "Are you going to stick with that God awful orange-colored shoe you seem to always like or will you broaden your horizons?"

"Honestly, I'll probably go with the black and white Nike shoes here." Alex grabbed a box of the Nike FS Lite III shoes and took it to the register. Once they bought the shoes, they set out for McDonald's. Alex hated it, but Hailey couldn't live without it.

"Hey, I'm going to run to the bathroom okay?" Hailey said when they walked in.

"Yeah go ahead, I'll just order your usual. Yes, I know what it is, because you eat this garbage like it's going out of style."

"Oh, shut up." Hailey laughed as she walked to the bathroom. Alex waited in line, just to see his ex-girlfriend Sandy as the cashier. So, naturally, he did what all guys would do; he decided to man up and slip a note under the bathroom door and wait for Hailey in the car.

"What the hell happened, Alex?" She asked when she got back to the car.

"Hey good news honey, we are going to the drive-thru. Sorry, there was a line inside; too long for me."

"Uh, okay, that's fine, but we are the only one's here so I doubt-"

"Oh hey look, no line in the drive-thru."

"Welcome to your Wendle McDonalds, how may I help you?"

"We will have a number two with bacon and a root beer and a number ten with no mayo and a Diet Coke."

"That'll be $9.60 at the window, thank you."

"So what do you think, fat girl mid-twenties or teenager with psychological issues? I vote teenager." Alex said. This was a crude game Alex invented for when he and Hailey were in the drive-thru. Loser has to pay.

"God, you are such a child Alex."

"So you concede? Do I win again?"

"No. I got your ex-girlfriend. Check mate mother fucker."

"No way. She's-"

"Hey look at that, good job Hailey, you won." Alex turned to see Sandy smiling in the window. "$9.60 Alex, pay up."

"Shit, how?" Alex kept looking back and forth between Hailey and Sandy in shock.

"Well, when I saw the note, I walked over and saw her. She said you ran out like a little bitch, so I decided to have some fun with it."

"Collusion." Alex gave the money to Sandy and took the food. He and Hailey ate in the car before he dropped her off at her car. It had been about an hour, so he went home.

Upon pulling into his driveway, Alex saw a car he had never seen before in front of the garage, which was odd on a Monday. It was a blue 2002 Lexus. He got out of his car and went to look in the windows to see if he could tell who it was, but nothing. Just then he heard two loud gunshots from inside his house. He grabbed his dad's old .44 from the garage workbench, loaded it and ran in the front door. When he got inside he saw a stranger holding a smoking gun and standing over his mother and sister, both shot dead.

Alex and the stranger both raised their guns. Alex got three rounds off in the stranger's chest before he could get one off. Both Alex and the now dead man collapsed to the floor. One from three bullets, one from pure horror and shock. Alex crawled over to his mother, trying to hold back tears. It didn't work. He broke down and began crying. He grabbed his mom and sister and hugged their lifeless bodies, lying there in a pool of their still warm blood, heartbroken and dead inside. As he grasped them he wanted to call the cops, but the only thing he could think about was the last words he said to her.

"*I'm so sorry Dad, I failed you*," He whispered as he felt his mother's limp body grow cold.

Chapter 2: The Trial Part 1

Two weeks after the death of his family, Alex was set to appear in court. He was a suspect the murder of all three of the victims at the house that night. Although he was all but cleared of any involvement in the murders of his mother and sister, he was being investigated thoroughly about his involvement in the murder of the other man. What made this case all the more important, was the fact that he was being tried as an adult.

Inside the courtroom, Alex stood with his family lawyer, Dave Hinsdale. He had been their lawyer and friend since Alex's father passed away, dealing with all of their issues, creating wills and making sure they were happy. He and Alex had grown close over time, and nobody felt worse for Alex than he did.

"All rise," the court officer instructed, "the honorable Judge Mike West." The judge made his way into the crowded courtroom, scanning the room with his eyes as he took his seat. He was aware of the situation Alex was in, and he personally felt sorry for him. He had to keep that contained, however, because as the judge on the case, he needed to be unbiased.

"This court is now in session," Judge West said, bringing the mallet down. "We are here to review, dissect, and get a full understanding and timeline of events that occurred during the tragic triple homicide on June 10th,

2015. The three victims were Debra Underwood, age 39, Becky Underwood, age 14, and Darren Blackstone, age 26. A moment of silence for them."

The court stood still. Everyone in the room remained silent for fifteen seconds, the longest fifteen seconds of Alex's life. He looked up and saw a number of individuals: The family of Darren, the man who killed his family; his grandparents on both sides of his family; the jury, and the judge. Finally, Judge West broke the silence to begin the case.

"Let's begin. Mr. Hinsdale, please step forward and begin." Mr. Hinsdale looked at Alex. The two exchanged a reassuring look. After everything that had happened since the death of Alex's father, he knew he couldn't fail Alex in this.

"Thank you, Your Honor." Mr. Hinsdale stood up and adjusted his tie. "Ladies and gentlemen of the jury, I don't want to take too much time here so I will just lay it out for you. To say that my client took the life of Mr. Blackstone is fair. It may look that way, but to assume that he murdered his own family? To even consider that idea would be bringing up far more pressing issues than a murder. I have known Alex for a while now, and he has never been one to have an outburst or a short fuse. Mr. Underwood sits here before us with no previous records of violence or hatred towards his family or others. Now, to further prove his innocence in the murder I have brought in the local blood spatter analyst from the police station. What is your name sir?"

"Uh, Bill Fields," The man on the stand said.

"And what would it be that you do in your job?"

"I work as a blood spatter analyst for the local police force. I am the man who investigates crime scenes based on the pattern of blood spray and age of the victims to determine what happened. I was the lead investigator on this particular case."

"Please explain your findings to the court Mr. Fields."

"Well, Mr. Blackstone was found with two bullets in his chest, both from a Glock .44 pistol. A third bullet from the same gun was found in the southeast wall, at an angle that suggested that his shooter was standing near the front door while shooting. Mrs. Debra Underwood had one shot from a 9 mm Glock pistol in her head, and Ms. Becky Underwood the same. There is significant blood spray on the southwest wall, painting a clear image of the shooter being taller than the two victims, and standing near the southeast wall. While Mr. Underwood's fingerprints were found on the Glock .44 pistol, no fingerprints were found on the 9 mm Glock pistol. So unless Mr. Underwood shot three scattered and shaky shots at Mr. Blackstone, put on a pair of gloves, stood on a chair and then changed direction to shoot two perfectly precise shots in his mother and sister, I see no possible situation in which Mr. Underwood killed his family."

"So you believe he did kill Mr. Blackstone, correct?" Mr. Hinsdale said, changing direction.

"In self-defense, yes. The evidence shows three shots in scattered places, one going clean through the stomach, one in the left rib cage and one near the right shoulder. Mr. Underwood took gun training and safety class with his father last summer, the only way he would have been so inaccurate is if he were caught off guard, panicked, or was in danger himself. I do believe Mr. Underwood killed Mr. Blackstone, but I also believe that if he hadn't, we would be having a whole different conversation."

"Thank you, Mr. Fields. That'll be all Judge." Mr. Hinsdale went back to his seat and awaited a response from the judge, "I think that went well, Alex. Hopefully the jury sees things as they are, and not as the other guys try to paint it."

"Mr. Strange, it's your turn." Tyler Strange was the lawyer hired by the Blackstone family to make sure Darren's image stayed intact, by any means necessary. They had met Alex before; in fact, they really liked Alex and felt sorry for him, but the only way to prove their son's innocence was to prove Alex's guilt, whether true or not.

"Thank you, your honor," Mr. Strange said, standing up from his chair. He was one of the better lawyers in the state, and he acted like it. Most often compared to that of a snake, Strange had slicked-back black hair and always had a smirk on his face, as if things always went his way; which they did. "And thank you, Mr. Hinsdale. I would not go as far as to say you helped my case with your defense, but you certainly gave me something to go off of. I would like to call Alex

Underwood to the stand." The whole room gasped and fell silent in unison, waiting for the next move.

"Your honor, I object this is completely uncalled for," Mr. Hinsdale shouted, slamming his papers on the desk.

"Sit down, Mr. Hinsdale, you've had your turn. I'll allow it. Mr. Underwood, please take the stand for Mr. Strange.

Alex got up and walked to the raised chair next to the Judge. He had thought that this could happen, but he was in no way prepared for it.

"So Alex - can I call you Alex?" Mr. Strange said, condescendingly.

"Yeah, I guess." Alex was frightened of what he had up his sleeve. Whatever it was, it wasn't good.

"So Alex, on this day, why weren't you home?"

"I was out with my friend and girlfriend for a while, I don't know what that has to do with-"

"Yes, Alex that is what you were doing, but *why* were you with them? Why were you not at your house helping you mother clean?"

"We got in a little fight before I left, nothing serious though."

"All right, fair enough." Mr. Strange rubbed his chin, pacing the floor, "What do you know about your sister's social life Alex? Are you two - I mean were you two close?"

"Yeah," Alex was getting irritated, "we were. She was an angel before that animal broke in our house and murdered her."

"You shut your damn mouth!" Mr. Blackstone yelled from across the room. An uproar begun as the crowd debated whether the comment was called for or not.

"Order in the court, now!" Judge West smacked the gavel until the crowd went silent. "Please continue Mr. Strange."

"Thank you, sir. So Alex, the part of that I don't understand is that you say you were close with your sister. If you truly were, you would have known about her drug problem, correct?"

"Her what?"

"You see I did some researching and I found something very interesting; your sister had developed a strong dependency for marijuana. Her dealer, of course, none other than Mr. Darren Blackstone himself."

"There's no way, she was an angel she would never do that."

"Yet after your father passed, she did. In fact, if what I found is accurate, it started the day he passed, outside of the hospital. Alex, I realize this news may be shocking, but what I'm about to tell you and this great jury is sure to blow your mind. You see, Darren didn't force his way into your house. There was no sign of forced entry, so he was let in by someone. My guess is, your sister owed him some money, and he came to collect."

"Fuck you, you don't know that, you are just assuming that is what happened. There is no evidence that my sister or mother put up a fight at all."

"I'm glad you said that Alex, because if no evidence that they put up a fight proves he killed them in cold blood, then what does it prove since there is no evidence he put up a fight against you putting two rounds in his chest? I believe you killed him before he had a chance to kill them. You saw a gun in his hand and shot him. Your family was in shock, your mother screaming at you, and you took all of your pent-up anger and killed them. You killed them with his gun and gloves to frame him before you called the cops." Mr. Hinsdale buried his face in his hands, shaking his head in disbelief. "That will be all, Your Honor." Mr. Strange walked back to his seat with the same smirk on his face.

"Jurors, I will give you time to come to a decision. Our Bailiff will show you to conference room D." The jury left the room with the Bailiff. To say Alex and Mr. Hinsdale weren't optimistic would be an understatement, "Mr. Hinsdale, you and your client can go to conference room A to relax while the jury makes their decision."

Alex and his attorney made their way into the conference room where they would wait for the verdict.

Mr. Hinsdale stepped out of the room for a while to make a few calls, leaving Alex alone in the room with his thoughts.

The chairs were meant to be comfortable, but they weren't. Not in the slightest. Cold steel. That's all he could feel, the cold steel of the hard chair and the somber gray table. He knew that positive thoughts would help, but it wasn't easy. He struggled to see any positives in his situation. He was prepared to get ten years in the state prison for manslaughter and murder in the first degree. After about twenty minutes, Mr. Hinsdale entered the room.

"Well Alex I've done the best I can but it doesn't look good." He wiped the sweat from his forehead. "The good news is they are aware that the man killed your mother and sister, so you are cleared of those charges, but the bad news is you still killed him. We made a strong self-defense statement, but that certainly fell apart with Strange's interrogation. You doing all right, Alex?"

"Yeah, I'm fine." Alex knew he wasn't fine, but containing his true feelings is what he did best. "What do you think the verdict will be?"

"Well, it's tough to say, but I think you will be in it deep either way. Best case scenario, the jury understands your situation and gives you a break. Worst case scenario, you get 35 to life for murder."

"What else was I supposed to do? He killed them and was going to kill me next, it was my only choice," Alex was terrified at the thought of him going to prison for being in the wrong place at the wrong time, "if they were in this situation, they would all have done the same thing."

"All we can do is hope they see it our way. There's still a chance you could get off with just probation and a slap on the wrist. Possible, not probable." They heard a subtle, yet firm couple of knocks on the door. "That was quick. Maybe even a little too quick."

"What does it mean?"

"It means they were all in agreement on what to do." Mr. Hinsdale wiped the sweat from his forehead again, walking towards the door.

"Do you think that's a good thing?"

"No," he said as he opened the door.

"Mr. Underwood, they are ready for you," The Bailiff instructed from the door. Alex and Mr. Hinsdale looked at each other.

"It means we are fucked, Alex." They made their way out to the desk in the court to hear the ruling.

"Welcome back, Mr. Underwood," The judge sighed and looked up at Alex. "Before the verdict, I would just like to say that whatever the punishment is, I am truly sorry. We all would have done what you did, and it is unfortunate that you are in this position. Jury, have you reached a decision?"

"We have your honor. After reviewing the case and evidence brought to our attention by both Mr. Dave

Hinsdale and Mr. Tyler Strange, we find the defendant Alex Underwood, not guilty of first-degree murder, not guilty of manslaughter, and guilty of second-degree murder. Mr. Underwood found Mr. Blackstone who murdered his family in the act and proceeded to act in what he viewed as self-defense, killing Mr. Blackstone."

"Thank you jury. Mr. Underwood you should be extremely grateful. Under these circumstances, you will be charged with a 90-day house arrest, spanning from tomorrow, July 1st, through September 28th, and will be fined $10,000 by the federal government, which can be paid in monthly intervals of $216 over the next two years, paid by either him or his current guardian. Failure to pay a monthly fee will result in 60 days in prison. I will also assign an officer to keep an eye on you for these 90 days, partly for your safety and partly for others. An ankle bracelet will be applied for the 90 days as well. It is up to you and Mr. Hinsdale to decide where you will be spending the 90 days, with my approval required, of course. Congratulations Mr. Underwood." Alex sat with his face in his hands to mask the tears rolling down his face.

"Excuse me," Mr. Hinsdale interjected, "Honorable Judge West, is Alex going to be able to attend school for his senior year? I believe that if he is free of charge, he should be able to mingle with his peers."

"Interesting point. In exactly one month's time there will be a vote in this very room, the teachers, officers, city, and especially parents of the students who attend the high school will vote on whether Mr. Underwood will be allowed back in school. That could be a tough vote, so I will encourage all who can attend, to attend. Case dismissed." Judge West left the room as murmuring and chatter flooded the already tense air.

Upon leaving the courtroom, Alex's grandparents on his dad's side, the rich ones, approached him to take him home with them. They were, in all sense of the word, assholes. If they didn't need you for something or you couldn't go to see them on your own time, they had no use for you.

"Hello Alex, are you ready to go home? You will need a place to stay while you are on house arrest." Mr. Underwood said.

"We have a lot of chores for you to do so you can make enough money to pay the monthly fees," Mrs. Underwood said. Alex tried to say something but was cut off by Mr. Hinsdale.

"We are not sure where Alex will be staying right now," He put his hand on Alex's shoulder, "and until we figure it out he will be staying with my wife and me."

"Actually, no, I am going to stay with-"

"Us. You are staying with us whether you like it or not, Alex." Alex was cut off by Mr. Underwood, "We have the most resources to provide you with a comfortable life."

Mr. Hinsdale grabbed Alex and pushed through them. The decision had been made, and if the Underwoods wanted custody of Alex, they would have to wait. His other grandparents, the Carlisles, saw him from a distance and ran up to him. They were much happier and family oriented than the Underwoods.

"Alex! Oh we are so happy for you!" Mrs. Carlisle hugged Alex with a smile, "Thank you so much for everything Mr. Hinsdale, you have been so great for this family."

"Thank you, I am just doing what's best for Alex. Now if you could excuse us." Mr. Hinsdale tried to get Alex out of the building and back to his house. With both grandparents trying to get Alex to go with them, they had to get out of there as soon as possible. Mr. Hinsdale rushed Alex outside.

When they walked out of the building, media and crowds suffocated him with questions and pictures. Alex saw Andrew on the sidewalk at the side of the building. He found his way out of the crowd and to Andrew, abandoning Mr. Hinsdale. He had gotten out of the trouble and away, just to see Mr. Strange on the other side.

"Congratulations Alex, you got off. Your mother and sister would be proud," He said with the same slimy smirk as per usual. Alex walked up to him, clenched his fist and brought him down with a right cross, breaking his nose.

"You don't get to talk about them you son of a bitch!" Andrew pulled Alex back and got him into the escort car before media could get to him. Alex knew it was stupid, but it felt so good.

"You little shit!" Mr. Strange yelled as Alex got away, "You're fucked kid, you hear me? Fucked!"

Chapter 3: On the Run

Andrew and Alex got away in the car and went back to Andrew's house. Mr. Hinsdale had been trying to call Alex, but he wasn't going to answer for a few hours. He knew that Mr. Hinsdale would be angry, and he had enough of the arguing and turmoil for one day. Alex and Andrew didn't talk much on the ride to his house either. It had been quiet until Andrew broke the silence.

"Well I gotta say Alex, that was pretty stupid," He said, shaking his head. "Punching him like that might hurt your case to go back to school."

"I doubt it. If he presses charges I'll be charged with aggravated assault, maybe a few extra money charges, I can handle that."

"Was it worth it, Alex? Like really, was it? Do you have any idea how serious this situation is?"

"Look, maybe it wasn't the right place or time, but it was the right thing to do. That piece of garbage needed to get knocked down a few pegs."

"I agree, but you should've let me do it; you don't need to be in more trouble. Oh hey, where were you going to stay for the time being, did you decide?"

"I figured I would just stay here with you, is that cool?"

"Yeah, no problem, I'll let my mom know and we will fix up the guest room for you."

"Ok cool, I'm going to walk down to the gas station, you want anything?"

"No thanks, catch you later."

Alex started walking down the sidewalk towards the gas station. He heard his phone ring and took it out, just to see Mr. Hinsdale calling again. Soon he would answer, but not yet. Alex noticed a black car had been creeping down the street behind him for a while now, letting cars pass it. He shrugged it off, though. He figured it was just another guy obsessing over him and the case.

At the gas station, Alex grabbed what he wanted and went to check out. The man at the register had always been a little weird to Alex, but of course now he was especially odd. He had a lazy left eye and an eye patch on the right. He watched as best he could as Alex walked out of the store.

Walking back to Andrew's house, Alex quickly went from a light stroll to a brisk power walk to a run when he noticed the black car still following him. He ran as fast as he could back to the house. When he got there, he locked the door behind him as two men got out of the car.

"Jesus Alex what the hell is going on?" Andrew asked, coming into the room.

"Stay here and don't let them in, I am calling Mr. Hinsdale." Alex took his phone out and called him. The men approached the door. Behind it stood a nervous Andrew, confused about what it was he was supposed to say. The men knocked at the door.

"This is Officer Lannister and Officer James; may we speak to the owner of the property?" The first man said. Andrew struggled to find the right words.

"Uh sorry, she's at work, come back later," he finally got out.

"Not an option, son," the second man said, "we have reason to believe a Mr. Alex Underwood is inside, and we have a warrant for his arrest. Open the door kid, make this easier on all of us."

"Alex, what do I do?" Andrew whispered in a panicked rush.

"Just stall, okay? I'm figuring it out." Alex had finally gotten connected to Mr. Hinsdale on the phone, and he was not happy.

"Alex, what the fuck! Where were you?" Mr. Hinsdale yelled into the phone upon answering it. "I've been trying to get a hold of you for hours now. What's this I hear about you assaulting Mr. Strange?"

"I'm sorry, but I needed to get away from everything for a while. Look, Mr. Hinsdale, Andrew and I are in it deep right now at his house. Two men followed me and claim to be officers who have a warrant for my arrest."

"Shit... Shit, okay, um have they shown you the warrant? I'm sorry, there is only so much I can do over the phone."

"No, we won't let them in yet."

"They aren't inside? Great job, tell them they need a search warrant to enter the house. If they enter without one, and without consent, you are off clean. They will need to order one from the station and that will take at the very least thirty minutes, which should give me enough time to get there and drive them away."

"Okay, hurry." Alex hung up the phone and started pacing the floor.

"What do I say?" Andrew whispered.

"Tell them they need a search warrant or you'll sue the county."

"Officers, do you have a search warrant? If not, I will press charges if you enter the house." The two officers went silent and answered a few minutes later.

"We have ordered a search warrant on this house and it will arrive here shortly. Once it arrives, you have no choice but to let us in. Until then we will watch the house to make sure nobody leaves." Officer Lannister called out.

"Alex, what is happening? Is Mr. Hinsdale coming?" Andrew called to Alex across the room.

"He will be here soon. As long as he gets here before the warrant we should be fine."

The two pairs sat on opposite sides of the door waiting for their respective package to arrive. Whichever made it there first would walk away from this on top. After a half hour, a car finally pulled up.

"Hey Alex, some car just pulled up," Andrew said, drawing Alex back into the room.

"Who is it?"

"I don't know, the windows are dark and they haven't gotten out yet."

Outside, the two officers were having a similar conversation about the vehicle and its mystery driver.

"Is that a car from the station?" Officer James asked.

"I'm not sure; if it is, it's not one I've ever seen." Out of the car came Mr. Hinsdale, paperwork in hand.

"Officer Lannister, my name is Mr. Dave Hinsdale. I am Alex Underwood's attorney and I am here to tell you that your accusations are false and not backed by legitimate evidence. You and your lackey need to get off this property and do not return unless you have actual evidence that my client has assaulted Mr. Strange."

"Actually, Mr. Hinsdale, we do have evidence. He showed up inside the courthouse with a broken nose claiming your client hit him. He has ordered him to be arrested, so we are here to collect him."

Mr. Hinsdale fell quiet, trying to come up with a way to counter that argument. Meanwhile, a second car showed up, along with the search warrant.

"Officers," the intern from the office said, running out of the car, "here is the search warrant."

"Thanks Jack, you did good," Officer Lannister commended him before taking the papers. "Mr. Hinsdale, here is a search warrant, now get your client to open the door."

Mr. Hinsdale hesitantly walked to the door. He had no idea how to go about this. Why would Alex do that so soon after the ruling? Why would he risk a re-trial?

"Alex, Andrew, it's Mr. Hinsdale, they have a search warrant, please open the door," he said through the wood and glass. The door opened slowly, as the officers burst through to arrest Alex.

"Alex Underwood, you have the right to-" Officer Lannister looked around the room to see Andrew wearing Alex's clothes, but no Alex.

"Where is he kid? We know he's here," Officer James commanded.

"I'm sorry guys but he's not here, he's never been here. It was me you saw at the gas station. I'm sorry I ran, but I was scared you were coming for me," Andrew responded.

"Why would we come for you?"

"Because it was me who punched Mr. Strange. He was antagonizing Alex behind the court and I knew Alex would snap so I hit him and we left. He swore he would pin it on Alex, which is why you are here." The officers looked stunned and were at a loss for words.

Andrew stood his ground, insisting that Alex wasn't in the house and that it was him who broke Mr. Strange's nose. Meanwhile, Alex sat in the kitchen listening to the conversation. He knew it was just a matter of time before they would go to look around in the house for him, so he decided to head for the back door. He accidentally knocked a glass off the counter, signaling the people that he was in the house. Officer James burst past Andrew and drew his gun as he entered the kitchen.

"Ground, now!" He looked around the empty room and was dumbfounded, "Sir, he's... He's not here."

"Where the hell did he go then? Obviously *someone* was in here a few seconds ago, so find out where he went!" Officer Lannister marched over to Andrew in anger.

"I told you, he's not here." Officer Lannister grabbed Andrew by the collar and brought him in close.

"Until we find him, you're going to be placed under arrest for assisting an escape." the officer commanded while placing handcuffs on Andrew.

"He has confessed guilt, and in court that will hold up over a claim any day of the week," Mr. Hinsdale interjected.

"I did it, not Alex, take me," Andrew pleaded.

"I know you're just doing this to save your friend. He did it, not you. Now you will serve time for a crime he committed. It will be on your record forever. Think about that.

As they took Andrew to the car, he looked down the street to Alex's house where he could see him hiding under the deck. He thought about ratting him out to the cops.

"Okay, fine it was him. He did it. Now he's over there, under the deck of his house. Hurry, he's going to run," he said as Officer James sprinted towards the deck. Alex saw this and ran, but didn't make it. The officer took him down, breaking three ribs and dislocating his shoulder. The officer smashed Alex's face into the concrete, shattering his teeth. Andrew screamed, trying to get him to stop, but the officer wouldn't let up.

That's what would've happened. That's what should've happened. Andrew knew that, and that's why he said nothing. He knew it was best that he take this and hope Alex stays out of trouble while on house arrest for the 90 days. The officers took him down to the station. Andrew was booked and sentenced to be in the county jail for the next month before the second trial. Alex was to stay at Mr. Hinsdale's house for the rest of the house arrest, with the only exception being the trial.

Chapter 4: The Trial Part 2

One Month Later

On the day of the second major trial, Mr. Hinsdale sat in the waiting room with Alex as they awaited the arrival of Andrew. He had been refusing to take any visitors or calls for the last month while he was in jail, so they hadn't spoken to him since the incident back at his house.

"I don't know what the hell is taking them so long to bring him out," a frustrated and anxious Alex said, "they said today they would release him and it's almost 3 P.M., why is he not out?"

"Don't worry Alex, he will be here." Mr. Hinsdale reassured him without looking up from the list of names expected to speak at the trial.

Not long after, the court officer escorted Andrew into the waiting room. He looked rough. Scars on his hands and face, and a pretty thick layer of stubble for an 18-year-old.

"Andrew," Alex proclaimed, rising from his chair, "Jesus Christ you look terrible."

"Thanks man, means a lot." He said, walking past Alex and straight to Mr. Hinsdale, "Add my name to that list Mr. Hinsdale, I want to give my piece."

"Should I be concerned, Mr. Streeter?"

"No, I just have a few things I need to say. See you in there." Andrew and Alex exchange hard looks as Andrew leaves to go to the courtroom.

"What the hell was that?" Alex said, turning to his attorney. "Is he going to try something in there? Did they get in his head?"

"No, I made sure he was kept in protective custody after his first fight. No officers or inmates messed with him, I don't know what's going through his head. He's had a whole month by himself to think, though, and that's never good."

"Well, when we are in there, make sure he is in check. No stupid shit today."

"Got it, no stupid shit." Mr. Hinsdale joked.

They made their way into the courtroom for the trial. Alex experienced one of those moments that you feel will never end and everyone is staring at you. As he looked to his left he could see his mother's parents, Mr. and Mrs. Carlisle; the happy ones. They saw him and waved, smiling as they did. He looked right and saw his father's parents, Mr. and Mrs. Underwood; the rich ones. They were in formal attire and paid almost no attention to Alex as he came in, almost as if this was more about them than him. Looking straight forward he could see Andrew, Judge West, the court officer and the superintendent of the district, Mr. Browning.

"Ah, welcome back to society Mr. Underwood," Judge West said, "I guess we can get started now. Everyone, please be seated."

The court was in session. On the table for this trial was the judge giving his final decision on who Alex would live with, and for people to voice their opinion before voting on whether to let Alex back into the public school system or not. The final decision would be determined by the vote, but certain aspects could be altered by Judge West if he felt it necessary.

"All right, let's begin with the custody rights." Judge West searched his desk for the papers. "Mr. and Mrs. Carlisle. You believe that you are best suited to be the guardians of Alex because, for the time he has left as a minor, you can provide him with a, and I quote, 'safe and happy environment, like that of his old family' correct?"

"Yes your honor," Mr. Carlisle stood up and straightened his tie, "unlike that of the Underwoods, we will do our best to ensure Alex is as happy as humanly possible. Money doesn't buy happiness."

"That's horseshit!" Mr. Underwood shot up out of his chair. "Without money you have-"

"Order in the court!" Judge West commanded, smacking down the mallet. "Now that's enough Mr. Underwood. If I recall, you believe you and your wife are best suited to be the guardians because you can provide him with, and I quote, 'anything he could ever want, with money and luxury' correct?"

"You're damn right. With how much money we have, there is no way he couldn't be happy. Hell, to celebrate, we will take a trip to Bora Bora for a couple of months." Mr. Underwood sat down following his speech.

"Well, I have come to a decision. While I do hate taking away anyone's rights to family, I have to choose one. With that being said, I am awarding full custody rights of Mr. Alex Underwood to Mr. and Mrs. Carlisle, effective immediately following the trial. As they are now the guardians, it is up to them when Mr. and Mrs. Underwood can see Alex. Now, let's begin on the next part of the trial. We will all be taking part in a vote on whether or not Alex

Underwood will be allowed back into the public school system. Before the vote, however, everyone will be given the chance to speak their mind on the subject if they want. So, who would like to be the first to speak?" Judge West gave the floor to the rest of the court. The first to stand up was the superintendent of the district.

"My name is Harold Browning and I am the superintendent of the school district. As Alex has been a student in my schools for a while now, I have been following this situation closely. While I will be keeping my vote a secret, I will say that if Alex is allowed back to school, he will be welcomed with open arms from us here." He sat down as the room applauded him. The judge asked if anyone else wanted to speak and the room went silent. Nobody spoke up.

"Thank you Mr. Browning. Next up." The second person to speak was a parent of a student that went to Alex's school.

"Hello, I'm Stacy Darling, and I am a mother of two, one a fellow classmate of Alex Underwood at school. They have been in school for years together, and, while they have never been too close, I do believe they are friends. With that said, I would not feel comfortable with my son sitting next to a murderer in a classroom, regardless of the situation. If he returns to school with my son I will demand that they not have any classes, sports, or lunches together. I imagine he's a sweet boy, but I won't have him near my son." She made her way back to her seat, dodging piercing stares.

"Thank you for your input Mrs. Darling. Is there anybody else who would like to speak?"

"Uh yeah," Andrew got up from his chair, "I would."

"Ah, Mr. Streeter," Judge West said, settling back in his chair, "I forgot you were released today. How was the county jail?"

"Cold." He replied with a glare that could kill a moose. "Like our honorable Judge here referenced, I did spend the last month in the county jail for assaulting the lawyer Tyler Strange following last month's trial. In school I am the ideal student, straight A's, no missing work, great athlete, I'm going to Stanford University, not even any discipline on my record. That is, until now. Why did I do it? Why did I ruin my perfect record for my friend? Because Alex is my brother. I would take a bullet for him. Hell, I would jump in front of a speeding car for him if I had to. The point is I would do anything for him, especially now. I am voting yes, he should go back, and you all should too." Andrew walked back and took his seat.

"All right, if that's everyone, I guess I will speak." Judge West cleared his throat, "This case is special to me. Not because I can relate; I can't. It's special to me because I want this young man to receive justice and peace in this unfortunate situation he is in. I'm not sure how this vote is going to go but I do know that I will definitely be voting for Alex to continue his education alongside his classmates in their senior year of high school. You all will vote the way you will, but I encourage you to think about what I said. Let's begin the vote."

As the court officer handed out small sheets of paper to the crowd of people in the room, Alex felt as if he couldn't breathe. He wanted back into the schools. He wanted to finish his education with his friends, but he knew that it wasn't up to him. He couldn't vote. There were 83 votes that would be submitted, including one from the superintendent, the parent, Andrew, the judge, and each of his grandparents. After about 30 minutes, the votes had been collected and counted.

"Thank you for your patience." Judge West said as he returned to his seat. "I have counted the votes submitted and we have come to a verdict. In the decision of whether Mr. Alex Underwood is to be allowed back into the school system, the vote has come back as 48 for, 35 against. Based on comments written on the cards and the people who spoke before the vote, I have decided to change the manner in which Alex will return to school. Alex will attend the first day of school like usual, and will graduate with his class, but he shall be homeschooled for the days in between. He is welcome to attend as many days as he wishes, however, there will be no penalty for any missed days, so long as he turns in all assigned work."

The courtroom erupted into a loud cheer as the crowd left the room to celebrate. Alex, however, did not want to celebrate. Though he was happy, he just wanted to go home. It was finally normal, and his life was back to normal. Or so he thought.

The media was swarming around Alex and his new guardians. The constant flashing lights and questions quickly went numb to him and he couldn't hear or see anything. His grandmother guided him to the car and they drove away as Alex came back.

"What the hell happened?" Alex got up from his laying position to look out the window.

"It's okay honey, we are going home. The media were too much, hopefully they respect our privacy and leave us alone."

We. Our. Us. Alex hated the sound of these words almost as much as he hated his grandparents. He hated both of them, his dad's side and his mom's. One was too attentive, the other not enough. He secretly didn't want to be with either. His new guardians used these words like they were struggling with the situation too. That pissed off Alex more than he could explain.

Chapter 5: The First Day Back

For the first time since the incident, Alex slept without experiencing horrific and unnervingly realistic nightmares outlining what could've happened. He had been having these for so long, it was to the point that he would expect them every night; however, in the absence of those, he had dreams of him killing people. People he didn't know, people he did know, anyone. He felt no remorse, almost as if he felt he was doing the right thing.

On the morning of his first day back to school, he woke up two hours before he had to actually get ready. He sat on his bed thinking about all that had happened over the last few months. He couldn't get the image out of his head of his mother and sister lifeless on the floor. He had never thought about it before, but how was he supposed to return to society? To *school*? Most of these people he hadn't seen for months, and he knew that they wouldn't look at him the same. Hell, when his father died, nobody talked to him at school for days. Not even some teachers. What was going to happen now that his entire family was dead, and he had killed someone? Was anyone ever going to talk to him?

"Alex?" His grandmother had walked in the room. "Honey it's 4 A.M., what are you doing up?"

"I'm fine, I just couldn't sleep. Could I have some time alone please?"

"Okay dear, just let me know if you need anything. Oh, by the way, we are going out to eat at that pizza place we like today if you want to come." Alex silently shook his head as she walked out of the room, leaving the door open behind her. That was another thing, they didn't like having any closed doors in the house. Alex couldn't quite figure out if it was a privacy thing, a space thing, or a trust thing, but either way he hated it. He didn't like having his door open. He wanted his personal space, especially after all that had happened.

After a few hours, it was time for him to leave to school. The first day of his senior year. The first time he had seen a lot of the people since the incident. He didn't know if he should be scared, sad, nervous, or happy. So he was all of them. Because he was still on suicide watch, as the court orders for all traumatic incident survivors, he was still not allowed to drive a car. He couldn't drive to school, and he sure as hell wouldn't let his grandparents drive him, so he walked.

The mile long walk to school was one of the more peaceful moments he had had in a long time. The trees were at that point where they weren't quite turning like they do in the fall, but you could tell they were almost there. The air still felt warm, because it was still summer, but there was a nice fall breeze that was weaving in and out of the trees and buildings. For the first time in a long time he was happy. For that brief moment, he escaped the insane world around him. That feeling was gone quickly, however, as he turned the corner and walked into the school yard.

Have you ever had a time where you feel like everyone is staring at you and time stands still? Alex hadn't. Not until that day. As he entered the school yard, he felt like the whole world stopped spinning. Everyone stopped what they were doing and stared at him. Birds stopped chirping, frogs stopped croaking. The only sound was the eerily muffled whispers like you'd hear from a crowd at a golf match after a golfer misses a putt. It seemed like everyone was in the yard, all staring at him. He knew everyone was talking about him too. That was the worst part. That small yard seemed miles long, and seemed to take forever to get through as he crossed to the front entrance.

The hallways weren't much better. The only real difference being that people couldn't slowly move away from him as they talked about him, so he could hear some of the whispers.

"Oh my God, I can't believe he actually came to school," they'd say, "are you going to avoid him? I am. I can't talk to someone who has *killed* a guy!"

He felt anger. He wanted to grab them and beat them until they didn't have a mouth to talk out of anymore. He had never felt that way before other than in the dreams he had before. It scared him. He turned into Mr. Crow's class. Mr. Crow was his favorite teacher last year and managed to get him again for his senior year. Mr. Crow immediately got up and locked the door behind him, then grabbed Alex and hugged him tighter than he had been in a while. Alex broke into tears. All the emotion he had held in for the last three months all came out at once.

"Alex," he said, "when I heard what happened I wanted to try and get into contact, but I was advised by your lawyer, Mr. Hinsdale, not to until school started up again. Look if you need anything-"

"It's okay Mr. Crow, I'm all right," Alex said. Mr. Crow knew as well as Alex did that he wasn't all right.

"Are you sure you'll be okay with being here today? You know it's going to be a rough day."

"I don't want to dwell on the past like that; it's over, I want to be able to finally move on with my life. Hopefully school will help me with that. Besides, it's a required day for me to attend, it doesn't matter if I want to be here or not."

"I know." Mr. Crow sat down in his chair, "Well, Alex, I hope you do all right today, let me know at any time if you don't. Anyway, I'll see you in 6th period." Alex nodded and walked out and down the hall.

He had gotten fairly lucky with his schedule. Art with Mrs. Thatcher 1st period, followed by history with Mr. Jeplin. In the past, he had been in class with both of them and had a good time. After that, his schedule got a bit tougher. Math with Mrs. Hyde was next. She was a complete bitch to everyone. Even the teachers hated her. She had even be donned the nickname "the Führer". In 4th period, he had French with Mr. Dupont. He wasn't a bad guy, in fact he was a lot of fun in class and during extracurricular activities, but he was a terrible teacher. 5th period was science with Mr. Crest. He was new to the school, so nobody quite knew what to expect. Last was English with Mr. Crow. They had connected the year before, and had been close ever since.

Alex had made his way to the art room right before the bell. When he walked in, everyone stopped and stared at him again. Mrs. Thatcher slowly made her way over to him.

"Good morning Alex," she reluctantly said, "you can have a seat in the front here." She led him to his seat as if he were a blind cat. This was something he knew he would have to get used to, at least for the day. He sat down as they started class.

As Mrs. Thatcher started class, Alex could feel all eyes on him. With his back to the class, too scared to turn around, he could assume that he was the center of attention, not the teacher. After she noticed the lack of attention to her lecture, she gave the class a task.

"Okay class, get out a sheet of paper." Mrs. Thatcher walked over to her desk and got a drink of water. "I want you to draw a sketch of the best day of your life. Due at the end of the period. If you would excuse me for a minute." She walked out of the room. It was clear to the class that she was not happy, and most would assume at least part of the reason had to do with Alex.

"What do you think is wrong with her?" Kate, the girl behind Alex said to her friend Brittany.

"I don't know," Brittany lowered her voice to a whisper, "I think it's about Alex though. I know I wouldn't want him in my class after what happened. I don't even feel safe having him *sit* near me."

"I know what you mean," Kate said, also whispering, "I thought he was cute, but after he killed someone... No way."

"What do you think Hailey will do? Break up with him?"

"I hope so. For her safety."

Alex ignored them. He knew that they, however ignorant, were right in a way. He had been ducking Hailey for months, and hadn't talked to her since the day she got back in the summer and they spent the day shopping together, the day everything changed.

He tried to think of a happy day to draw. He came up with the last time he went camping with his family, even his father. One sure way to make any of them happy was to go camping, which they did several times a year. This trip was special in his mind, though, as it was the last time he would see his dad healthy.

After about twenty minutes of awkward silence and drawing, Mrs. Thatcher returned. She called Alex up to her desk with a note in her hand.

"Alex, the counselor wanted to see you. He said that you should take your bag and everything with you." She said to him at her desk. Alex grabbed the pass and his bag and left the room. It was fairly obvious to everyone that she had done something to try to move him out of her class, but nobody said anything.

He walked down the hall towards the counselor's room. Alex couldn't help but think of Hailey. He needed to see her, to talk to her, but he didn't know where she was or if she even gave a damn.

He didn't have to look too hard for her, though, because as he turned a corner, there she was. She was leaving her biology class to go to the bathroom and they happened to run into each other. He pulled her out of the school and into the old storage building where kids would often go to have sex and do drugs.

"Alex, I haven't heard from you in months," she let out a sigh of relief, "I honestly thought you had just forgotten about me. After I heard what happened and-"

"No, I don't want to talk about that," he stopped her, "look, I'm fine, but I just want to forget about it. I am sorry I didn't call you or anything, it has been a tough few months. But still, like I said, I'm ready to move on."

"You can't just forget about that stuff... It's who you are now. It sucks, but it's a part of you and always will be."

"It doesn't have to be."

"Yes it does. Until you can fully accept and get past what happened, you will never be truly okay. Everyone has a breaking point Alex, even you."

"Are you not even fucking listening to me? I *am* over it. I *am* okay. The only thing bothering me right now is you. I am trying to be happy and move on with our lives but you seem to want to just keep me in this emotional limbo and I don't want that."

"Hey, you can't talk to me like that."

"I'm sorry, Hailey I really am. I think I need some space. I don't want to, but I think we need to be done." Alex kissed Hailey on the forehead as she began crying. "I do love you, and I'll always be around for you." Alex walked past her and continued on his way down to see the counselor.

Once he got there, his assigned counselor, Mr. Trager called him in.

"Hey Alex, welcome back," he said with a smile, "how's your first day going?"

"Everyone is staring at me, nobody will talk to me, but they will whisper to their friend right next to me, my teacher doesn't want me in class and I broke up with my girlfriend of a long time, how do you think it's going?"

"I suppose it's not the best day, no. I'm sorry Alex, I wish there was something more I could do to help you. Perhaps after a few days back-"

"Don't worry, I've already made up my mind. I won't be coming back after today; I'll do the work at home with my grandparents. I don't need to be here, I'm just a distraction."

"Oh, are you sure? Alex, it may not be the best idea to leave so soon. You should confront your problems head on."

"Don't use your counselor mind tricks on me, ok? You did it last year when I tried to get out of chemistry too and held off talking about it until it was too late for me to switch out, I know your tricks. I like you, I'm sure you're a good guy, but I was given the option on whether I wanted to come back after today and I am going to have to say thanks but no thanks on that one." Alex shook Mr. Trager's hand and left. The bell rang as he left the room, so we made his way to his next class to continue his first day back.

Chapter 6: Worst Day Ever

After a less than stellar 1st period, Alex prepared for the worst in the rest of his classes. His 2nd period, history with Mr. Jeplin was better than he had expected. He was called on for an answer twice and even talked to a couple of friends. Following his 2nd period, he happened to run into Andrew in the hall.

"Hey Alex!" he called from down the hall by the vending machines, "what class are you going to?"

"I'm on my way to math with the Führer, should be fun. What about you?"

"English with Crow. You talk to him this morning?"

"Yeah I stopped by. I have him 6th. What do you have 4th and 5th?"

"Uh French with Dupont and math with the Führer. What about you?"

"I got French with you, then science with Crest. Have you heard anything about him? I hear he's new. Nobody seems to know who he is."

"Yeah, I had him in 1st period. He's all right, seems a little too laid back though."

"I hope he's not like that for my class, I like easy teachers, but too easy isn't fun, you don't learn anything." the bell rang, interrupting their conversation, "Okay, well I'll see you in 4th."

"Good luck with math." Andrew laughed as they parted ways.

Alex and Andrew went to their respective classes, Andrew a little more excited about his class than Alex. When Alex entered the class, the Führer did her best to make him feel welcome.

"Seriously?" she sighed in frustration, "I thought I told them I refused to teach you. Fine, until I can get this cleared up, sit at the back desk."

The Führer had never been nice to Alex, or anyone for that matter. She was in every sense of the word, a bitch. Nevertheless, he was shocked at how brutally honest she was being this time. He could tell that Mrs. Thatcher was uncomfortable with him in class, but at least she didn't come out and say it in front of the class like that.

"You know, Mrs. Hyde, I don't have to come to class," Alex said, "I mean, nobody wants to come to your class anyway. So I could very well just say fuck you and leave."

"Mr. Underwood, I will not have that kind of language in my classroom. I am going to ensure you are removed from this class as soon as possible."

"Really? Wow, thank you Führer. I mean, I was going to say that I won't be here in school after today, but not having to do work for your class is a bonus!" Alex sat down in his chair and paid no attention to any part of the class. After all, he wasn't a part of the class anymore.

After class, Alex met up with Andrew for French. He was pretty excited to tell him the good news out of the Führer's class.

"Andrew, man, you won't believe it," Alex ran up to Andrew as he entered the room. "I actually got the Führer to pull me from her class!"

"No way you must be kidding," Andrew laughed in disbelief, "nobody *ever* gets the pleasure of getting out of her class. It's almost like she enjoys making our lives hell and torturing us."

"I don't know how I did it, but yeah I really got out of her class. How was Crow today?"

"Not bad, but I don't like the way he teaches. I never really have though, he's a little too eccentric for my liking. I know you do though, so you'll probably like it."

"I don't know how you don't like him, he's by far the best teacher in this school."

"If you say so." Andrew put his stuff down and took a seat next to Alex. The two continued a conversation for a few minutes when Hailey walked in.

"Uh-oh," Andrew said looking past Alex's head to the door, "trouble to the south."

"What?" Alex turned around to see Hailey surrounded by guys. They had just broken up earlier that day, but like he had expected, she received immediate attention.

"You want to deal with that?"

"No," Alex responded, brushing it off, "why would I? I broke up with her, I should expect it. She's absolutely gorgeous, she will get attention."

"Okay, man, but just remember, if you want to take someone out, I got your back." Andrew joked as the class started.

Mr. Dupont was a quirky teacher to say the least. Extremely socially awkward. It was a wonder to everyone how he had been a teacher for so long. To start class, he had everyone say something to someone in French. Alex thought hard about what to say, and settled with "J'ai fait une erreur, j'ai encore besoin de vous. Je t'aime." Or, in English, "I made a mistake, I still need you. I love you." He planned on saying it to Hailey, as he had been rethinking his decision to break up ever since he did it. The first man up was Carter. He and Alex used to know each other more, but grew apart over time. He decided to say something to Hailey as well.

"Hailey," Carter said, "Irez-vous au retour à la maison avec moi?" Hailey's face lit up with excitement.

"Of course I'll go to homecoming with you Carter!" Alex's heart sank. He looked at Hailey and they locked eyes for a second. A second that went quickly for her, as she embraced in a hug with Carter, but a second that lasted a lifetime for Alex. He knew that any chance he had to get her back was gone now. In that one second Alex went from heartbreak, to anger, and then to a feeling of being sick. He looked at Carter, wanting to tear him apart right there, right now. In front of everyone. That was his girl and had been for years; he couldn't let her get taken away so soon after he mistakenly left her. Alex got up from his seat and started towards Carter. Andrew sprang up and grabbed Alex.

"Mr. Dupont, can I go to my locker?" He shot out, "I left my French dictionary in there. I forgot my combination from last year so I need Alex to come with me to help."

"Absolutely Mr. Streeter," Mr. Dupont unknowingly agreed. The fact was that he didn't have a locker that he shared with Alex. Nobody had lockers, it was the first day of school, but Andrew had to get Alex out of there.

"What was that Alex?" He asked, pulling him into a nearby bathroom.

"I don't know, something came over me, I just-"

"Let's never do that again, okay? I thought you were done with her?"

"I know I thought I was but I just can't see her with someone else that soon." Alex washed his face off in the sink.

"Well what were you going to do if you had gotten your hands on Carter? If I hadn't of been there?"

Alex punched the mirror, sending a majestic web of cracks throughout the once shiny sheet. He didn't say anything, but he turned around to see Andrew backing away from him into a wall.

"Andrew, I'm fine, seriously, you don't need to back away from me like that."

"No Alex, you're different. You have never been like this, I don't know what's come over you lately but it's scaring me. Figure it out man, please. I don't need you going off the rails."

Andrew walked back to the classroom, leaving Alex in the bathroom by himself. He didn't want to admit it, but Andrew was right, he was different. There was something eating away at him inside that was making him think and almost do unthinkable things.

Alex got himself cleaned up and made his way back to the classroom to finish the class. Since he could never say what he had planned on saying to Hailey, he got special permission from Mr. Dupont to be skipped over for this assignment. For the rest of the class he sat and listened to the class talk in French, saying nothing to Andrew or anyone else.

The class ended with the bell, sending them all off to lunch. Before Alex could get out the door, however, Mr. Crow came into the room.

"Alex? The office needs you right away, you have to come with me." Mr. Crow said to Alex. The two set off through the massive traffic jam of people in the hall towards the office. Mr. Crow wouldn't tell Alex what it was about, but he assumed it had to do with the mirror.

On the way down, they passed the library. There were two guys standing outside talking. They turned their attention to Alex when he appeared.

"Hey Johnny check it out, it's Batman!" Mike said, "the man who got vengeance for his family's murder."

"No way! I thought it was a myth! Should we ask for an autograph?" Johnny laughed.

It was at that moment, that everything went dark for Alex. He saw red and lashed out. Alex pushed past Mr. Crow. threw his backpack at Johnny and ran for Mike. Everything past that was a blur until it was able to get broken up by two security guards when they pulled Alex off of the kids.

"Alex what the hell are you doing?" Mr. Crow said, pulling him off of an unconscious Johnny, "It's your first day back and you're already doing this?"

He didn't reply. He just kept silent. He looked around and saw what he did. Johnny was sitting on the ground against the wall with blood pouring from his nose, and Mike was unconscious on the ground, with a broken nose and blood all over. For that moment, whatever had been inside him since the incident had taken over.

"Take him down to the office guys," Mr. Crow ordered, as he tried to help the two kids.

Two security guards walked Alex the rest of the way down to the office. They sat him at the desk, giving him hand sanitizer and a small towel to clean the blood off of his hands. Principal Murphy walked in and sat in her chair. She looked at Alex with a look of heartbreak and remorse.

"Alex, I called you down here today to discuss a developing situation that directly affects you, but now I'm not sure whether I will be able to talk about it with as much sympathy as I intended. You assaulted two of your classmates, why?"

"They were making jokes about what happened, am I supposed to just ignore that?"

"Well, I imagine they weren't the first to do it, and they won't be the last. Why them? Why now?"

"I had something that was bothering me, so maybe that influenced what happened."

"You know, I think you're probably right, Alex. Well, I heard about your decision to not return after today and I also think that is the best thing to do."

"Glad you see it my way. Now why did you call me down here? What happened?"

Principal Murphy took a drink of water and used a handkerchief on her desk to wipe off her mouth and face.

"Alex a few hours ago there was a crash in downtown Wendle. A van had its brakes go out driving down a hill towards the downtown area, a Honda van I believe it was."

"That's terrible, but why does it affect me? Nobody I know drives a van."

"The man driving the van was the lawyer Tyler Strange. That was the lawyer opposing you, correct?"

"Yeah that's right. He was son of a bitch too." Before Principal Murphy could respond, Alex's phone starts ringing.

"Could you get that later Alex?"

"No sorry, it's my lawyer Mr. Hinsdale; I need to get this now." Alex answered the phone and wasn't able to get a hello in before Mr. Hinsdale started talking.

"Alex it's a shit show down here have you heard about the crash?" He said into the phone with urgency.

"Yeah just a bit ago, why?"

"It was Strange who was driving the van, he died immediately. His van lost its brakes and crashed into a restaurant, that Italian place on the corner, eight inside died. Alex, there's more. There was a letter inside the van addressed to the court. He was going back to appeal their decision to pin the assault on Andrew and not you."

"Wait, the one with the amazing pizza? Where we went a few months back?"

"The very same. I'm sorry, Alex. I'm so sorry." Alex hung up the phone and buried his head into his hands.

"Alex, what happened? What's wrong?" Principal Murphy asked.

"The van was thrown by th- the bus," Alex struggled to get the words out, "it went into the Italian restaurant. Killed eight people."

"Why is that so bad for you?"

"Strange had a letter he was taking to give the court; it was in the van. He was appealing the court decision to convict Andrew and not me. My grandparents were eating there today. They are dead because of me." Alex got up and walked out of the office. He left school and started walking down the road with no intention of going anywhere at all.

Chapter 7: Darker Days

Alex walked for about three miles before being picked up by Mr. Hinsdale outside of a Taco Bell. As Mr. Hinsdale approached him in his car, Alex sat on the curb, watching cars go by.

"Alex," Mr. Hinsdale said as he got in the car, "I'm so sorry. The last thing I wanted was for you to go through something like this again. Either way you should never have walked off like that, you should have waited for me to get you at the school or just finished the day."

"Sorry to disappoint you Mr. Hinsdale," Alex said sarcastically.

"We need to head back to my place to figure out just what the hell is going on and what our next move is."

"Why do we need a move exactly? My grandparents, the last people left who loved me died in an accident that only happened because I let my only true friend go to jail for a month for something I did. I have ruined the lives of everyone who has ever gotten involved with me, leave now or you may end up getting a life sentence because of me."

"Damn it, Alex, that is enough. You are not the cause of all this, okay? Bad things happen to good people all the time, you just so happen to draw the short straw quite often."

"It doesn't matter anymore. Let's just go, I'm done talking." Alex and Mr. Hinsdale sat quietly for the rest of the ride.

After a tense thirty-minute drive, they arrived at Mr. Hinsdale's house. The two got out and went inside. Mr. Hinsdale sat down a stack of papers and sat down on the couch while Alex did his best to do anything but what Mr. Hinsdale wanted to do.

"Alex get in here; we need to talk." He commanded.

"Fuck you Dave, there's nothing to talk about."

"Alex there is a lot to talk about. The accident, the appeal, how the judge will respond, repercussions, what's going to happen with your grandparents..."

"Fine, you want to talk?" Alex came into the room and sat in a chair, "you got my full attention and cooperation for fifteen minutes, then I want to go to Andrew's house, okay? I am so tired of this shit. I want it over. Done. But it just keeps dragging on and you seem to enjoy it. So you want to talk? Talk."

"Okay," Mr. Hinsdale let out a big sigh, "the city is taking the van in for inspection to make sure it wasn't tampered with."

"Do you think it was?"

"Honestly, at this point I would believe anything. I think the entire situation is a little peculiar and there may very well be a lot more to the story than what we see, but right now, until proven otherwise he was on his way to the courthouse, his brakes failed and people died. Do you think they were tampered with?"

"There is no doubt in my mind they were tampered with."

"You sound pretty sure," Mr. Hinsdale said, intrigued, "why?"

"He was furious with me after that day at the court and even more so when we countered his accusation with a confession, he wanted to get back at me so he followed my grandparents and made it look like an accident."

"Wow, that is a, uh, pretty big statement," Mr. Hinsdale laughed in amazement, "let's keep that one on hold for now, don't want any unnecessary attention."

"Okay, what about my grandparents, what happens to their bodies?"

"There will be a joint service held for them, your mother and your sister. I don't know when, but when I find out I will be sure to let you know."

"What about the killer? Does he get a service? He shouldn't be allowed a service. If they have one, it should have to be from inside a damn prison."

"I know how you feel about him, and you have every right to, but the fact is he didn't intend to kill them and he had a family of his own who loved him. He was a good kid and deserves a nice sendoff. Besides, it's more for his family than him. He will get one, I'm not sure when it is though."

"Fine, but I don't want his grave to be anywhere nice. Make sure they put it in a corner."

"No worries Alex, I will do my best." Mr. Hinsdale gave him pat him on the back with a laugh. "Come on, let's get you to Andrew's."

The drive to Andrew's house was much more pleasant than the one to Mr. Hinsdale's. The two listened to music and discussed the upcoming election and how they wanted it to go, though their opinions couldn't have been more different.

When they got to Andrew's house, Alex got out of the car and went inside after saying goodbye to Mr. Hinsdale. He walked inside and saw Andrew sitting on the couch.

"Well, you had a terrible day huh?" Andrew joked as he got up from the couch, "come on, I got a pizza in the oven."

"Oh hello, Alex," Andrew's mom was in the kitchen, "you boys are probably busy with something but I just wanted to let you know that you are always welcome here. Always."

"Thank you Mrs. Streeter." Alex and Andrew went into Andrew's room to play a game. If there were two things that could take everything off of Alex's mind, they were soccer and video games. Alex and Andrew played both religiously, and they were unbelievably good at them.

"What are you thinking? Fifa? Madden?" Andrew asked.

"No, I'm thinking Call of Duty. I want to shoot some stuff."

"All right, sounds good," Andrew agreed, although he was in a way uncomfortable with the way Alex had said it, given all that had been happening.

Watching Alex play the game wasn't too reassuring either. From his vice like grip, nearly breaking the controller in half, to the lack of talking he did, which was far from the usual. Whenever the two had played a game, any game, Alex was always the one to trash talk and gloat about what he did. Andrew was not against it by any means; in fact, he did his fair share of trash talking, but he certainly didn't like it when Alex did it constantly. This time, however, he would've taken the worst trash talking Alex had to offer over the eerie silence he was producing today. Andrew was more than happy to interrupt their game when he heard the oven time go off for the pizza.

"Oh, hey that's the pizza." Andrew got up from the chair and started out towards the kitchen. "Pause the game, we can come back later." Alex put down the controller and followed Andrew out of the room.

"What kind of pizza is it?" Alex was picky about his pizza, he didn't like any vegetables, and he only liked certain meats.

"Hawaiian. Your favorite." Mrs. Streeter already had the pizza out by the time they had arrived in the kitchen. "Oh, and Alex, Mr. Hinsdale called and wanted me to let you know that they have decided that they will finally go ahead with your mother and sister's service, it will be a joint service with your grandparents this Thursday."

"Thanks for letting me know. Mr. Hinsdale and I had talked about it earlier, he said that he would let me know when he knew when we were having it, I guess you're a more reliable person to pass information on to."

"Oh Alex, you know I am. Oh hey, by the way, I almost forgot, I was thinking that on Thursday, after the whole thing is done we can head up to Washington and go camping, does that sound like fun to you guys?"

"Hell yeah!" Andrew showed a lot more enthusiasm than Alex, but both were happy to go. It would be nice to get away for a while. Besides, it had been a while since either of them had been up in Washington. They lived in Wendle, a small town in Oregon. Less than 10,000 people lived there, and even less choose to stay. Every once in a while, just as a bit of an escape, Alex and Andrew would head up the Olympic National Park in Washington and go camping for the weekend. Sometimes with Alex's family, sometimes with Andrew's. Their favorite spot was a little known campground called "Seal Rock" on the Hood Canal. One of Alex's favorite family memories happened there.

It was the summer of 2014, and Alex's father, Christian, just got a huge pay raise at work. The four of them had gone up to Seal Rock to celebrate for the weekend. Alex's mom, Debra, was the type who always had a list for everything. So, like usual, she made a list for the trip. It included all of the camping essentials: tents, sleeping bags, food, water, and clothes. She did, however, make one mistake in the mad rush to pack. She forgot the tents.

None of them had realized until they had already made the six-hour road trip and began unpacking. The three-day trip was condensed to one night because of it. Nevertheless, what started out as a complete disaster turned into the greatest memory Alex has of his family. Laying there together and sleeping side by side under the stars. It was also the last time he had been there.

This was what Alex thought of when he heard that they were going up there at the end of the week. So, while he was happy to go back, there was a bit of hesitation before agreeing to go. He was resting on the hope that Thursday's service would bring enough closure for him to be able to enjoy the upcoming weekend.

Chapter 8: The Service

On the day of the service, Alex was nervous to give his speech. He hadn't been told that he would have to give a speech for sure, but he had a pretty good idea what was going to happen once everything got started. He knew that many people there would be crying the whole time, unlike him.

There was no denying that Alex was upset about his family's passing, but it was clear his way of coping was far different than most people at the service. From the moment he stepped out of the car door, he was drowning in hugs and well wishes. Alex was never much of a hugger. Nobody he knew well would ever hug him, and he didn't like someone, often someone he either barely knew or didn't like, constricting him with their entire body. The good thing about Alex, though, he was an incredible actor. He could fake a smile better than Brad Pitt himself. He had decided that it was probably better to play to the crowd for the service, so that they wouldn't be asking why he doesn't seem sad for three hours.

"How are you doing, honey?" Alex's aunt Greta came up and embraced in an uncomfortably long hug. "Oh I have just been crushed reading the stories and articles about what has been happening to you."

"Oh don't worry, I'll be okay." Alex managed to form a halfhearted smile while holding his breath to protect himself from her strong musk of thick perfume and cigarettes. Luckily for Alex, he didn't have to fake for long because the one person he could be himself around, Mr. Crow had just arrived.

"Hey," he maneuvered the crowd, finding his way to Alex, "you doing better? Last time I saw you, you weren't in a good way to say the least."

"Yeah I know, I'm sorry about that. I'm doing a lot better now though. Andrew's family will be taking me up to Washington tomorrow, so that will be fun."

"That's awesome Alex, it will be good for you to get away for a while. You'll still be doing your work though, right?"

"Of course Mr. Crow, for your class. You know, for a while I was actually kind of eager to go back to school, but everyone there treated me like I was another species. Some alien from a foreign planet. Like I was someone they had never seen before."

"In a way I had kind of expected that, but that doesn't mean it was right. It's too bad, Alex, I was really looking forward to you being in my class again, it'll be empty without you. Are you going to talk during the service today?"

"Yeah I had planned on saying a few words. Not too much though, I don't want to be the center of attention. Just enough to satisfy everyone enough so they won't pander me with annoying questions during the dinner after."

"Are you kidding me? You're the *only* person people actually want to hear. Nobody cares what your lawyer or family friends have to say, it's your opinion and feelings that matter. Look, Alex, just go up there and pour you heart out. This is your moment, embrace it and use it to really show them how great you are."

"Thanks Mr. Crow." Alex chuckled and shook his head as he walked away, thinking about what he will say. Despite what he had told everyone, he had not prepared anything.

"Excuse me everyone," Mr. Hinsdale, also the host, said out loud over the large crowd, "we are almost ready to begin the service. They are finishing the last service and funeral now and we will begin soon after that."

"Host, huh? How'd you land that gig?" Alex said sarcastically.

"I knew a guy," Mr. Hinsdale uncomfortably joked back with a wink, "it'll be a second though, they aren't done yet."

"Do we know who it was for?"

"No, I am not sure, I never saw the list."

"Wait a minute." Alex walked closer to the door to listen. He recognized the voices, he knew he did. The Blackstones. It was the funeral service for the man who murdered his family. Alex immediately saw red again. Mr. Hinsdale caught this almost immediately and pulled Alex away to the parking lot.

"Let me go, Dave, I'm fine," Alex screamed what he could of the sentence through Mr. Hinsdale's hand over his mouth.

"Alex, I swear to God I didn't know they were before us," Mr. Hinsdale said with urgency, "just calm down and let them do their thing."

"Oh don't worry about me, I said I'm fine," Alex definitely was not fine, and Mr. Hinsdale knew that.

"Okay, okay, well let's just wait out here until their service is over just in case, maybe you can go for a walk huh? There is a river at the other end of the cemetery, over the hill."

"Yeah sure, sounds good. Get me when it's time."

Alex grabbed a muffin from the stash of food for the dinner after the service and started walking towards the cemetery. Once he got over the hill and out of sight, he started to get an odd feeling, like someone was watching him.

"What is that, blueberry? Chocolate?" Alex turned around to see a guy around his age leaning against a tree, "mind if I have a bite?"

"I don't really know what it is and no you can't have a bite, who are you?"

"My name is Nathan. Shouldn't you be inside Alex?"

"How do you know my name? Why are you even here?"

"That doesn't matter. Here's the thing, people keep saying that the Blackstones had nothing to do with their son and what he did but you and I both know that's bullshit. I mean his mother *birthed* him for Christ sake. Shouldn't you get them back in some way?"

"I killed their son, I think that's punishment enough, even if he was who he was."

"No, no, it's not. You see, he will always live on through them, so if you think about it, he's not really dead yet, now is he? How did he become that way?"

"Some people are just sick. Some people just go crazy."

"Goddamn I have a lot to teach you," Nathan stepped closer and put his arm around Alex's shoulder, "we need to kill the Blackstones." He whispered in Alex's ear.

"Are you insane? That's the worst thing I could do. When they find them, who do you think will be the first person they look at?"

"And how do you think they will find them?" Alex looked down and saw a shovel laying on the ground. The church workers had prepared a grave for Darren Blackstone and had it empty and waiting for his casket. The only people set to be present for the casket as it went down were his parents. Nathan handed Alex a knife, patted him on the back and wandered off out of the cemetery. "Don't worry, I'll draw them out." He said as he left. Alex stood there, thinking about what Nathan had said. Maybe he was right. Maybe he should kill them. He stared down at the big hole, kicking a little dirt in while leaving it open for the Blackstones.

About a minute later, the Blackstones started walking through the cemetery, drawn out by Nathan. This was his chance. Alex crouched behind the tree and waited for the husband and wife to walk past. Once they did, he pounced. He hit Mr. Blackstone with the shovel, then his wife. Once they were both knocked out, he placed their bodies in the graves faced them down and cut their throat and vocal cords with his knife. Blood started spraying everywhere, like he had expected, so he threw in his sweatshirt with them. Using the shovel, he filled the holes with dirt and looked down at what he had done.

"There you go man! You see? Now you get it." Nathan appeared from behind the tree again. Alex didn't want him to be, but he was right. For the first time in a very long time, Alex was truly at peace, "You didn't take their money or anything, but it's okay, next time. Beginners struggles. Oh, hey Hinsdale is coming, give me the knife. Catch you later." Nathan took the knife and ran off. Alex started walking out of the cemetery and ran into Mr. Hinsdale.

"Oh, Alex it's time to start the service. Everyone else is gone, no need to get worried, you won't see the Blackstones. Hey, where did your sweatshirt go?"

"I got mud on it so I threw it away. Yeah I don't think we will see them anymore, I'm not worried." The two made their way into the building and everyone took their seats. Mr. Hinsdale walked up to the stage and the service started.

"Okay everyone, I'd like to welcome all of you to a very long overdue service. This is a joint service for Debra Underwood, Becky Underwood, Janet Carlisle and Dakota Carlisle. Let's all have a moment of silence for them." The room fell silent. Alex, standing in the back, looked around and saw everyone bowing their heads, no doubt saying prayers in their heads. Alex had never been the religious type. Definitely not the praying type, though.

"Our first speaker will be the son, brother, and grandson of the lost today. Alex, if you would please come up."

Everyone watched Alex walk down the aisle just as the kids did as he walked across the school yard on that first day of school. He didn't like it then, and he sure didn't like it now. He got up and stood at the podium, looking out at the crowd.

"I uh, honestly didn't prepare much. I have two quotes on this sheet of paper that I can connect with strongly that I wanted to share. The first one says 'My family is everything. I am what I am thanks to my mother, my father, my sister... because they have given me everything' spoken by Ronaldinho. Growing up in my house, there was always at least one argument going on at some point. Honestly, most of them were probably about something stupid, like dinner, or the television. Just stupid shit like that. But, looking back, it's that same shit that I miss. I would give anything to be able to argue with one of them. Just one last time. My second quote is by one of the wisest men to ever live. 'All the adversity I've had in my life, all my troubles and obstacles, have strengthened me... You may not realize it when it happens, but a kick in the teeth may be the best thing in the world for you.' Walt Disney. I stand here before you, and next to four urns that contain the ashes of people that I was laughing with less than 200 days ago, talking about their deaths. You can't anticipate the unexpected. You can't even be prepared for it. You just need to learn to adapt. I have learned to adapt. My mother is the greatest person I have ever known. She..." Alex looked down and watched a tear fall from his eye to the floor, "the last words I ever said to my mom were telling her I wish she was dead. Of course I didn't mean it, but I still said it. The thing that really gets me is I said it because she told me to wash the dishes while she was out. The dishes. If I could say one thing to my mom, it wouldn't be I'm sorry. It wouldn't be I love you. It would be thank you." Alex looked down again, and saw far more than one tear fall this time, "I'm sorry, that's uh, that's all. Mr. Hinsdale?" Alex walked off the stage and out of the church doors as people watched on in silence. He sat down on the brick wall of the flower bed and tried to pull himself together. Andrew followed him out and stood in the doorway. He didn't want to say anything to him until Alex had noticed he was there.

"How bad was it?" Alex asked.

"Pretty bad," Andrew joked, "not really, you did good. You showed real emotion and spoke from the heart, that's all we wanted."

"I guess I should've gone up there with a plan huh?"

"No way, it was way funnier this way." The two laughed, "come on, let's go back inside. Service will be over in a while."

Back inside, Alex stayed in the back of the room while others gave their speeches. One of Becky's teachers was there. She had a heart-warming story of Becky helping another student try to read in 1st grade. It was good to see all these people talk about them in such a good light.

Towards the end of the service, Mr. Hinsdale and Alex snuck out of the back to go into the dining hall.

"Thank God it's almost over," Alex let out a sigh of relief, "I thought we would be in there forever."

"Yeah I was getting hungry so I thought we could get a head start."

"So what kinds of food do we have cooked up here?"

"Just finger food and snacks," Mr. Hinsdale started working on an apple, "most people won't stay too long, calling it a dinner was just a formality."

People slowly started leaking into the room as the service ended. Alex got up from his seat at the table and moved to a chair in the corner of the room, in a sly attempt to not be noticed or bothered. He watched as everyone mingled, mourned and ate the food. He looked out the window towards the cemetery where he had killed the Blackstones and met Nathan. He wanted to know where he went, he wanted to see him again. There was something about him. Something drawing Alex back to him.

"Hey, how ready are you to leave?" Andrew said to Alex while eating a banana.

"Are you kidding me? I was ready to leave before we even got to step out of the car three hours ago. How long?"

"My mom just has to grab her bag and shoes and we will head out."

"Awesome, I'll meet you outside. I am going to let Mr. Hinsdale know that we are heading out before we go."

"No problem, see you there." Andrew tossed the peel in the garbage and walked outside. Mr. Hinsdale was still by the food table, so that's where Alex went.

"Hey, we are heading out soon, just wanted to let you know."

"Oh, awesome," Mr. Hinsdale said between spoonfuls of pudding, "do you know when you'll be back?"

"No I don't not yet. I think probably about four days we will be gone, maybe less. We get no cell phone service what-so-ever up there so I won't be able to check in."

"Ah, it's all right, I think you need a free weekend. Go on, have fun. It isn't like anything crazy is going to happen down here in little old Wendle while you are gone." The two laughed, but they wouldn't be laughing if they knew how crazy this next weekend would be for both parties.

Chapter 9: The Vacation

Alex didn't say much on the six-hour drive to Seal Rock Campground. Because they were driving at night, Andrew slept most of the way. Alex just stared out the window, thinking about what had happened in the cemetery at the church earlier in the day. He couldn't help but smile when he remembered the way it made him feel. The only question he was left with, was if he would ever see Nathan again. He wanted to. Nathan was smart and knew more about how Alex was feeling than anyone else.

"Alex!" Andrew started calling his name, "Alex, you alive?"

"Why wouldn't I be?" Alex glanced over at Andrew. He quickly realized it was morning. He had been staring out the window daydreaming for five hours already.

"I've been trying to get your attention for like five minutes now. Jesus what's wrong? You look like you saw a ghost."

"Sorry, I'm just really tired. How close are we?"

"About an hour out, maybe thirty minutes. Oh, and Alex, when we get there, my mom wants us to go find something to do. She doesn't want us to get in the way until she needs us to help set up." Mrs. Streeter had always been that way. She hated having people around while she unpacked and filled out the information for the tent site. Nobody really knew why, but at the same time nobody ever asked. That would mean getting in the way.

"Have you checked the weather for this weekend? I brought clothes for rain, not sun."

"No I haven't but it looks like rain. Besides, we are in the northwest, right up near the Hoh rainforest, it'll rain at some point in the next three days." It didn't. In fact, it was absolutely beautiful, aside from a morning dew on Friday and aftermath of a small shower Thursday night. That was the most important day of the trip for Alex, but we'll get to that.

"Oh hey, when is the season opener?"

"September 13th. Or do you mean your bitch of a team's opener?" Alex and Andrew both liked football; not as much as soccer of course, but they supported different teams. Being in Oregon, they were stuck in the middle between Colorado and Washington. Alex supported the Seahawks from Washington, and Andrew supported the Broncos from Colorado.

"Their opener is the same day dumbass. I wish the Broncos played the Seahawks again this year so they could kick their ass again."

"When exactly did the Broncos kick their ass in your lifetime?" Alex erupted into laughter.

"Yeah whatever," Andrew said, ending the conversation.

The two were fairly quiet the rest of the way to the camp. Once they got there, Alex and Andrew went down to the beach. They walked for a while down the beach before they saw a wooden bench. Alex stopped and stared at the bench.

"Hey, Alex, what's up?" Andrew went back to Alex, realizing he had continued walking while Alex had stopped.

"The last time I was here, I sat on that bench and had a really nice talk with my dad. We had come down here early in the morning on the day we were going home. We sat here for something like two hours."

"What did you guys talk about?"

"I don't remember anymore. Honestly, it doesn't even matter. I don't even think I knew what we were talking about at the time, all that mattered was he was talking."

"How long after that did he pass away?" Alex didn't answer. He turned around and looked out over the water at the land on the other side.

"I'm sorry Alex, let's just head back up to the camp, okay?"

"All right."

Andrew and Alex went back up to the camp and finished helping Andrew's mom set up, the camp. They would camp in tents, and not an RV like many people, because, as Alex's dad always said, "RV's are for hipsters, vegans, and pansies." That night, the two of them sat at the fire and talked about what had happened earlier.

"He died a few days later," Alex said, breaking a silence.

"Wait, what?"

"My dad. Earlier you asked me how long after the talk it was when he died. It was a couple of days later. He was diagnosed with lung cancer. I found out while at school one day. I got to talk to him before he died, luckily. I broke my promise to him."

"Oh my God, Alex I'm really sorry. I knew it was a cancer but…"

"It's fine, really. I'm over it."

"Alex, I need to ask you something and I need an honest answer, okay?"

"What is it?"

"What has been going on with you?"

"Andrew, I have no idea what you are talking about. What do you mean?"

"You know exactly what I mean. Your whole family has died and you have shown absolutely no emotion at all. What is going on?"

"I'm fine I don't know how many times I have to say that before you guys finally realize it."

"Everyone has a breaking point, Alex. You need to know when you've reached yours, or you'll be too broken to be picked up again." Andrew got up and went into his tent. Alex sat out by the fire for a while before retreating to his for the night.

Early the next morning, Alex got up and took the car to one of his favorite spots, Murhut Falls. Murhut Falls is a waterfall just south of Seal Rock that is a two-tier waterfall, meaning there is an accessible break about halfway down the falls. For those daring enough to do so, they could climb to the break and sit on the edge to look down the falls. Alex walked up the trail in his sweatshirt and thought about all that had happened and all that people had said. Was he at his breaking point? How would he know even if he was?

When he got there, he climbed up and sat on the edge of the falls, thinking about how nice it would feel to fall off, with the wind smacking him in the face right before the pillowy rocks gave him the release he had been looking for. He stood up and closed his eyes, listening to the sound of the falls. It was another sound that caught his ear though. A voice that seemed to be right behind him. He heard Nathan. He looked around, but didn't see him. It was so distinct, so sound that Alex thought there was no way it could've been in his head.

He didn't hear Nathan for real, however. Instead he heard a family walking up the trail. Not today, he thought. He climbed down and made his way back to the car before driving back to camp. Along the way he stopped at a gas station. He knew the tank was almost empty anyway, and he was growing pretty hungry.

"Hey there honey, welcome to the Brinnon gas station." The lady behind the counter greeted him as he walked in.

"Good morning," Alex greeted her with a smile, "where are your donuts and coffee?"

"Over there, right by the ice."

"Thanks." Alex walked over and grabbed a dozen donuts and a cup of coffee. The least he could do was get donuts for Andrew and his mom; not that he expected the full dozen to be there when he got back to camp. He walked up to the counter with the food and get the gas.

"That'll be $5.00 for the food." The lady said.

"Can I also put this twenty on pump two?"

"Absolutely." She took the money and went to set up the pump on the computer when a breaking news story caught her attention.

"Breaking news in Wendle, Oregon this morning as the parents of the deceased suspect in the Underwood family murder case were found buried dead in the grave meant for their son's casket. Currently the only suspects in this brutal killing are 18-year-old Alex Underwood, the lone remaining member of the Underwood family and his 45-year-old lawyer, Dave Hinsdale. Dave Hinsdale has been brought in for questioning by the police, and they are working hard to figure out the whereabouts of Alex as we speak."

"Oh that poor kid," the lady said, returning to the purchase, "he just can't catch a break. I bet the lawyer did it, trying to frame the kid. Slimy snakes those lawyers are. There you go, money is on."

"Oh, thanks." Alex tried to remain focused, "Do you have a phone I could use?"

"Sure thing, there's a pay phone right outside, just one dollar."

"Thanks." Alex ran out and called the Mr. Hinsdale on his cell phone.

"Hello?" He answered. "Who is this? I can't really be talking on the phone."

"Mr. Hinsdale, it's Alex, I heard about what happened."

"Shit, hang on." He fell silent for a few seconds before talking again, "Sorry, I requested to use the bathroom so we could talk."

"How did this happen?"

"I don't know, Alex. I don't want to know if you know who killed them, but they were killed with a knife. I need you to find the knife."

"How will I find it? It could be long gone by now."

"Just find it, Alex. Bring it here and they will see the fingerprints aren't mine. If they are yours we will find a way to get you off, if not, we are free."

"Okay, I'll try, just don't do anything stupid." Alex hung up the phone. How could things have gone that crazy? Because he was sloppy. He made it too easy to find the bodies. Alex went back to pump the gas and made his way back to the camp

He saw Andrew standing on the side of the highway at the entrance of the camp. He pulled up to see what was wrong.

"Andrew what are you doing?"

"Me? What the fuck are *you* doing?!"

"I just went for a drive; it's fine, nothing's wrong. But you need to hear what happened, the Blackstones are dead and-"

"Yeah, whatever. I don't know how I deal with you, Alex. I really don't. You're so afraid to feel anything that you shut everyone who cares about you out of your life." Andrew began walking across the highway to go on a walk of his own.

"Andrew, get out of the goddamn street, you're going to get hit by a car, they can't see you around that corner."

"You know what, no, you don't get to do that until you learn to have emotions. So I'm going to go on a walk, and when I get back, hopefully you have found the box you have had your emotions locked away in for so-" And everything went silent.

Chapter 10: One Year Earlier

One year earlier

"Hopefully I can teach all of you that reading William Shakespeare isn't the worst thing that will ever happen to you." Mr. Crow had just begun the lesson for the day when one of the student messengers from the office came in to deliver a message. "Alex Underwood?"

"Uh, yeah, over here," Alex nervously raised his hand. The school year had just started, but Alex could already tell his new teacher Mr. Crow would be a good one.

"Nice to meet you Alex, looks like you are needed in the office immediately. In trouble on the first day, huh? You going to be one of those kids who causes a bunch of problems?"

"Oh no, I am not like that at all Mr. Crow, don't worry." Alex got up from his chair to get the note from Mr. Crow and made his way to the office. Deep down, Alex really had a feeling he knew what was happening, but all he could do was pray that the feeling was not what was actually going down.

About two months prior to that day, Alex's father had been diagnosed with lung cancer. The doctors said it was untreatable, but he still had a chance. He had been in and out of the hospital ever since the diagnosis, but this time they didn't have their hopes up. Just days earlier, they were on a camping trip, the last of the summer. They would always hike as a family, but his father could barely walk this time. Once Alex got to the office, he saw his mother.

"Hey Mom, what's wrong?" Alex entered the room quietly.

"Alex..." his mother grabbed him and began sobbing, "it's your father. They say he won't make it through the day."

"No, no, Mom, not today please." Alex broke out into tears in his mom's shoulder as the two stood in the office.

"I know honey, I know, but sometimes things happen that we can't control. I'm so, so sorry Alex."

"Well, we need to go see him right now. Where is Becky? We need to get her and go up to the hospital right now to see him."

"Your sister is still at school; she can't know yet. Seeing him like that would destroy her. She is still too young, she wouldn't fully understand, but she would understand enough that it would break her for the rest of her life. There is no middle ground between serenity and the breaking point at her age."

"Okay, well then you and I need to go right now. I need to see him before he goes, Mom." Alex and his mom left for the hospital. Luckily, his dad was still there, but barely.

"Mrs. Underwood?" The doctor looked up from his clipboard to see an out of breath Alex and his mother. They had broken nearly every driving law in the book on the way there and had ran in, so they were a bit tired.

"Yes, that's me. How is my husband?"

"Well, I am sorry to say but he is really not good. I would say he has about an hour at the most, maybe less. If the two of you would like, we can let you both in so you can say goodbye and talk to him one last time before we have to prep for extraction."

Before the doctor even finished his sentence, Alex ran down the hall and burst into the room where his father was staying. He saw his dad on the hospital bed with what seemed like a hundred wires and tubes connected to all different parts of him. Alex didn't understand how they had gotten to this point. A few months ago they were happy and loving life, now, after such a long fall, they were faced with imminent death. His father was just 38 years old.

"Alex," his father said, "come here, please. I need to talk to you."

"Dad, I am so sorry. I need you." Alex started crying.

"Hey, we are Underwood boys, damn it, we don't cry." They both were fighting off tears. "I need you to hear me okay son? Not just listen, but really hear what I am about to say."

"Of course Dad, anything, what is it?"

"I need you to take care of your mother and sister, okay? You are the man of the house now. We all have jobs to do; that's yours. Take care of them. Your mother is going to have a tough time with this and your sister will be falling apart. You need to be there and make sure they keep it together. Can you do that Alex?"

"I promise Dad. I will do so good; I will make you proud."

"You already make me proud. You are going to go on to great things, Alex. I fully believe that. Life will deal you a bad hand, that's a guarantee, you just need to learn how to take it and make the best of it. Don't ever let it get the best of you. I love you son, so much."

"I love you too Dad," Alex and his father broke down into tears. He left the room to give his mother time with him. Alex was ready to step up and be the man he had to be, no matter what hand he was dealt. He could never let his mother do all this on her own.

"Excuse me, is this Mr. Underwood's room?" A man in a suit with a briefcase asked Alex, extending his hand.

"Uh yeah, why?" Alex looked him up and down, trying to think of who he could be and why he was here.

"My name is Dave Hinsdale, I am the lawyer that was hired by your mother to deal with the papers, coffin, and everything else for your father. I am really sorry to intrude on any moment you were having here, Alex, I was just looking for your mother. You are Alex, right?"

"Yeah that's me, it is a pleasure to meet you Mr. Hinsdale."

"And me, you Mr. Underwood. Hopefully we never have to do much business together. I like to make friends, but not in these circumstances." Mr. Hinsdale laughed at his joke. Alex did not.

"Alex?" His mother came out of the room wiping a tear from her face, "come up to the roof with me, I need to talk to you. Don't worry, Mr. Hinsdale I'll be right back to talk with you."

"No problem, Mrs. Underwood, take your time, I have no place to be for a while." Mr. Hinsdale sat down in a chair outside the room. Alex and his mother went up to the rooftop garden to get some air.

"Alex, can you do something for me?"

"Absolutely mom, anything, what is it?"

"I need you to tell your sister. Tell her to walk home today, we will be there later."

"Mom that's your job, I can't be the one to tell Becky that her father is dead, I have no idea how I would be able to do that or what I would say."

"And you think I do? Alex, my husband is dying. We are all going to have to step up and do things that are a little out of our comfort zone, can you do this for me? I really need you to step up from now on, okay? Promise me Alex, please. I have to go back down and deal with the lawyer I had to hire and I need you out of the way right now anyway."

"Yes Mom, I'll step up. I promise."

"Thank you Alex. I need to go talk to Mr. Hinsdale now. If you'd like you can stay up here until I'm done. I will be sure to come get you or send someone up for you."

"Okay, I'll be here." Alex sat down on a bench and looked at his phone. He knew he had to call his sister, but it was harder to do than even he had anticipated. Finally, he brought himself to dial her number.

"Hey Alex, what's up?" Becky said, "Are you picking me up or am I walking home today?"

"You, uh, you are going to have to walk home today Becky, sorry." Alex tried his best to get the words out.

"Are you okay, Alex? You are talking really weird, is everything okay?"

"Becky, it's Dad."

"No."

"I am sorry, Becky. I wanted you to be here but we couldn't let you see him like this."

"No."

"You saw him yesterday though, so at least you have a good memory of him." Alex waited for an answer. "Hello? Becky?"

She had hung up on him, and rightfully so. It was wrong of them to not bring her, and Alex knew that. He looked at his phone again and realized he had no one left he could or wanted to talk to.

Alex walked around the gardens a little longer before looking over the side of the building down to the streets below. He could see a group of gangbangers walking around causing trouble. He had no idea that someday soon, one of those simple gangbangers on the street, would change his life forever.

Chapter 11: The Accident

Alex heard nothing but white noise as the next several hours went by as a blur. He ran back to camp and got Andrew's mom. Together they went back to the highway to make sure Andrew was alive. The white Nissan that had hit him, now touched up with a thick coat of blood on the front still sat in the middle of the road. Andrew's mom went down to the gas station to call the paramedics while Alex and the man that hit Andrew gave him water, air and shade. The paramedics and police got there as quick as they could, but possibly not quick enough for Andrew.

"Okay everyone out of the way." The two guys from the ambulance rushed out with a gurney and carefully propped him up on it. "So what happened here exactly?"

"We were just up here and the car came around the corner and hit him." Alex barely got out.

"No way," the guy from the car proclaimed, "that kid was in the middle of the road man, I was between the lines, I couldn't get out of the way in time."

"Okay, well either way we need to get him to a hospital," said one of the paramedics as he prepared a few things to help keep Andrew awake in the back of the ambulance while the other got in and shut the door.

"What the hell are you doing, take him to the hospital!" Alex screamed as they appeared to be in no rush to leave.

"Sir, he is in critical condition, we won't make it in time. The only way to ensure he has a chance is to airlift him to Harborview in Seattle. I just called them and they have a chopper on the way right now, but we need the two of you to remain calm, you can meet us there if you leave now, we won't be able to put you in the helicopter."

Alex and Andrew's mom understood and got in the car to rush to Harborview in Seattle. Alex had to be the one to drive while Mrs. Streeter called everyone they could think of, including a few friends of Alex's like Mr. Crow and Mr. Hinsdale, if for no reason other than to let them know what happened. After an hour and a half, she was done calling people.

"Alex, what happened?" Mrs. Streeter asked with a less than optimistic tone.

"I have already told you, we were up there talking and the car hit him, that is it."

"Jesus Christ, Alex, cut the bullshit. I saw the car and where he was. The car was gone this morning and he was upset with you. What happened?"

"I'm sorry," Alex sighed, "I left early this morning to take a walk by myself up to Murhut Falls, for fun. When I came back he was there screaming at me. I tried to calm him down but he claimed he was going for a walk too and wandered into the middle of the street where the car hit him. I am really sorry; it is all my fault. If I had not left this morning…"

"No, Alex, don't pin this on yourself, it could have happened to anyone. He could have waited until you got back to camp. He could have walked down the side of the road and not through the middle. The guy could have not been driving today. So many things that did happen could have not happen, but the bottom line is they did, so we have to accept it and figure out what happens next."

The two of them were relatively quiet the rest of the way to the hospital. Once they had finally arrived, they were immediately brought to Andrew's room.

"How is he?" His mom asked the doctor.

"He's still in critical condition, but he is stable. He seems to have broken both legs and he has a severe fracture in his spinal column, which has temporarily paralyzed him."

"Do you think he will be okay? I mean, that's a lot to overcome."

"He should be fine in a few months or so, but we should be able to move him down to the closest hospital to your hometown in a week or so, and he will be free to go from the hospital a few days after that. If you could follow me, I have some paperwork that we will need you to fill out before you leave today."

She followed the doctor and Alex stayed behind to wait and see if he could be with Andrew. The thought of losing someone else close to him was too much to handle.

"Hey," Alex called out to a nurse who was coming out of his room, "is it okay for me to see him right now?"

"What is the relation?"

"For me and him?" Alex thought for a minute, "we are brothers." The nurse opened the door for Alex to go in. He saw the curtain wrapped around where Andrew's bed sat. He pulled it back and saw his best friend lying broken on the bed. Alex pulled a chair over and looked at Andrew.

"I'm so sorry, buddy," he said to an unconscious Andrew, "I promise I will make this right."

Alex sat next to his friend for an hour before Mrs. Streeter came in the room. She had just finished the paperwork to deal with the payments.

"How is he?" She asked as she set her stuff down.

"He is fine, still sleeping though. The nurse said he should wake up at some point in the next couple of hours."

"Good, good. Mr. Crow is on his way up right now; he should be here in an hour or so."

"That's great, it is good he can come up."

"What happened to Mr. Hinsdale, Alex?" Mrs. Streeter had not heard about the Blackstone murders yet, so she was surprised when Mr. Hinsdale could not come up.

"Oh yeah, I forgot you have not heard yet. This morning they found the bodies of Mr. and Mrs. Blackstone. They were murdered sometime yesterday. Right now, the primary suspects are Mr. Hinsdale and I. They have him in custody and are waiting for me to come in."

"Oh God. Did he do it?"

"No, there is no way."

"Are you positive? Surely there is no way you could have done it either, so who else?"

"I have no idea, we will have to see what happens."

Alex and Mrs. Streeter sat in the room for 45 minutes before Alex got a call from Mr. Crow saying he was in the building. Alex got up to meet him outside the room.

"Alex!" Alex turned around to see Mr. Crow running down the hall, "Alex, what the hell happened? Andrew got hit by a car?"

"We were camping. We had been arguing and he was walking across the street to get away from me. A car came out of nowhere and hit him. The corner is a blind spot but I didn't think…"

"It's okay, Alex," Mr. Crow pulled him close, "Andrew is strong, he'll make it through this, I promise. Where is his mom?"

"She is inside with him; we were in there for about two hours."

"What is the damage to Andrew?"

"Two broken legs and a severe fracture in his spinal column. They say in about a month he should be out of the hospital with a wheelchair."

"That is awesome, he got really lucky. The expenses must be crazy though, how much?"

"I have no idea; Mrs. Streeter would not tell me. She went over and signed some paperwork with the doctor when we got here, I imagine that had something to do with it. It's probably a lot."

"Yeah, she is a single mother who works over fifteen hours most days and barely makes it, she needs help. I'll go talk to them." Mr. Crow took off down the hall towards the doctor.

With Andrew's mom working just one job, and having to provide for her, her son, and now Alex, she was left with just $100 of non-essential money that would be spent on things like bills, gas, food, and car payments. $100 a month was not nearly enough to pay for what was bound to be an incredibly high hospital bill for Andrew. Alex decided the only way he could help her at all would be to get a job. Being out of school permanently would help in finding a job.

Once they had made it from Seattle back to Wendle, Alex spent the rest of the day looking for a job, but had no luck. The drug store wouldn't hire him due to the trauma he had been through, because putting him around drugs like that was "irresponsible". Wal-Mart wouldn't hire him because they didn't want him around guns. No restaurants hired him because they wouldn't hire killers. He knew it would be hard to find a job, he didn't think it would be impossible. He hated the idea of forcing Andrew's mom to pay for all of this herself, but there was no way for him to help. After he had given up the job hunt, he returned to the Streeter house where Mrs. Streeter was washing the dishes.

"I'm sorry, I tried. It seems my recent history is a bit of a turnoff to certain places," Alex said to Mrs. Streeter in her kitchen.

"Don't be Alex," she continued what she was doing, "you have been through too much these past few months, don't add my troubles to your conscience."

"I know I can help though, that is what kills me. You don't have enough money to pay for this, and I-"

"Damn it, Alex, that's enough," Mrs. Streeter turned around to face him, "I can figure this out on my own. You need to deal with your own problems. I know where my breaking point is, you don't. That's dangerous Alex. You need to figure out where it is and fast because once you're past it, there is no coming back."

"Okay Mrs. Streeter," Alex leaned in and gave her a hug, "I'll do my best, I promise." Alex left to try to find the knife he had used to kill the Blackstones. The first place he would check is the cemetery at the church where it happened. The last he saw the knife, Nathan was running down the hill towards the river with it trying to hide it, so that is where he went.

By the river were a number of rocks and holes perfect for hiding things of that size in, but there was nothing. He looked for a while before sitting on a rock and trying to think of where else he could look.

"Giving up already champ?" Nathan came up from out of nowhere to surprise Alex.

"What the hell are you doing here? Where did you put the knife?"

"Oh come on now Alex, we both know that we knew we were coming back to this spot to look for the knife. You can't help it, you need to do what you think the right thing is."

"Why do you say we were coming back?"

"What do you think I live here or something? No way, I just watch you Alex. I know you so much better than you think."

"Oh yeah? Prove it." Alex was standing up now, facing Nathan.

"Well, let's see. I know you left your girlfriend of two years because you wanted a break, and now you regret it because you still love her and she is with someone else. I know your friend Andrew is in the hospital and it is your fault. I know Mr. Hinsdale could be given a life sentence and it's your fault. And of course I know you are dangerously close to your breaking point."

"How do you know all that about me?"

"The how is irrelevant Alex, all I want you to know is I am here to help you reach your full potential. For you to truly embrace the insanity. For you to go far beyond your breaking point."

"Just show me where the knife is, Nathan. Let's start with that, okay? We can discuss the rest later when my lawyer isn't in jail for something I did,"

"Alex, you know where it is. It's safe. It's right where it is supposed to be. Lucky for you, the police should find it on their own before the day is done, so you can stop looking."

Alex tried to understand what he meant and ran off to the car. He took the car down to the station to see Mr. Hinsdale.

Inside the station, Mr. Hinsdale was still in a lone cell. Several officers threw Alex in with him almost instantly once he entered the building.

"Ah, thanks for joining us Mr. Underwood," Officer Lannister said with a smirk.

"Nice to see you as well, officer. How's the little partner over there doing anyway? Does he give good head? I can tell that is something you look for in a partner." Officer Lannister hit the bars with his stick.

"That's enough out of you, Underwood. We can have officers searching your car right now to see if you have the murder weapon in it. Is that what you want?"

"Sure, go ahead and look. Good luck with that Ponch." Officer Lannister gave him a hard look as two officers ran out of the building to search the car. They were gone for about five minutes before returning inside.

"We found it, there was a bloody knife sewn into the back of the passenger seat of the car. Underwood's car." Alex looked on in disbelief. How could Nathan frame him like this?

"Fantastic! Let's take a DNA sample of the blood and the fingerprints on the handle so we know for sure and we can book him for good." The officers took off down the hall with the knife.

"Why did you do it Alex?" Mr. Hinsdale asked, breaking the silence.

"I didn't, you have to believe me."

"I don't have to believe anything anymore." Mr. Hinsdale and Alex sat in silence as they waited for the results. After about fifteen minutes, Officer Lannister came back in the room.

"All right, let Underwood go. Someone get Mr. Hinsdale in cuffs and prep him to be transferred to Oregon State." He said with a hint of disappointment.

"What the hell is this?" Mr. Hinsdale commanded while being put in handcuffs.

"The blood came back as the Blackstone's blood, obviously, but the only set of prints on the handle were yours. I am thinking you got tired of Underwood's shit, planted the knife in his car and tried to frame him for murder. Smart. I am impressed. Good choice of victim too, but bad choice of town because we here are smarter than that."

"It was Nathan." Alex said to himself.

"What?" Mr. Hinsdale said as he was taken away.

"It was Nathan, he planted it, you were framed!" He yelled, but it was too late.

Mr. Hinsdale was taken down to the state prison while Alex was escorted out of the station and sent home. So Nathan had framed someone for murder, but it wasn't him. For some reason, even though his lawyer just got sent to prison to await a trial, Alex was glad Nathan did it.

Chapter 12: The Call

Following Mr. Hinsdale's arrest, Alex was sent to his other grandparent's house for a while. They were still unhappy over losing the case to the Carlisle's, so they were not exactly the most pleasant people to be around. Their house, however, was the polar opposite. It was, in every sense of the word, a mansion. It was a two story house containing six bathrooms, nine bedrooms and two kitchens.

When Alex arrived at the house, he was shocked at how big it actually was. He had never been to this house before, as he almost never saw his grandparents from this side of the family. For a two-story house, it looked like a castle. Vines covered much of the faded white walls of the building. A fountain sat in the middle of a round turn in front of the doors, with a moat jetting out from either side of the fountain and around the property. Since his grandfather owned a nearby golf course, their massive lawn was cut with a course licensed mower, cutting the grass perfectly in sync.

Alex approached the door and knocked, still in awe of how massive everything was. Even the door would be no issue for an eight-foot-tall man. Alex waited at the door for an answer for several minutes before wandering around the side of the house. Once he reached the back of the house, he finally found his grandparents.

"Hey, I didn't know you guys would be out here." Alex set his bags down and sat in a lawn chair next to his grandparents and waited for an answer.

"There is food in the kitchens to eat." His grandmother responded. "There is also a home theater, a one lane bowling alley, and an indoor swimming pool inside for you to have fun with. From nine in the morning until six in the evening we are not to be disturbed as we are very busy, after six we can socialize. Go inside, some guy is waiting for you."

Alex grabbed his bags and went inside to see who it was waiting for him. When he walked in, he saw a man in a white suit with slicked back blonde hair sitting on the couch. He looked young, maybe late twenties at most. The man got up when he saw Alex.

"Nice to meet you Alex, my name is Elijah Grant, I have been assigned to you as your temporary lawyer while the Dave Hinsdale situation is dealt with."

"Don't I get to choose my own lawyer? I'm not sure I like being assigned someone without having a say in it."

"Well I'm sorry Alex, if it helps at all I didn't get much of a say in it either. I have been following your story and to be honest, I am not a fan of you, Alex. I think you were dealt a shit hand, there is no debating that, but you are a little asshole too. I think you killed the Blackstones, not Dave. He was a good man and you ruined his life."

"I didn't ruin anyone's lives, especially not Mr. Hinsdale's life. He was my friend. If you are going to make accusations like that leave, I will find someone else."

"Look, regardless of how I feel, I am required to represent you. I can't back out of it, I was assigned to you. All I can do is do my best to get you free of the trouble you are currently in."

"What trouble?"

"Well, for starters, you assaulted two kids at your school the one day you went last week, so that is not good." Elijah got up and walked into the kitchen to get water.

"Shit I forgot about that. It was a momentary lapse of reason, it was a tough day anyway and they were, as much as I hate saying it and using it as an excuse, bullying me."

"Yeah, don't say that, it just sounds stupid. And either way, you were and are in hot water, you just can't be going around and punching everyone who pisses you off."

"Do you have any idea how we are going to get out of this?"

"Well it has been about a week and you have not heard anything yet, right?"

"Yeah, I haven't even thought about it since it had happened until you mentioned it."

"Then we should be fine, unless they are still talking about how to go about it. The other problem is the accident involving Tyler Strange."

"What happened with the van? I heard that it was going to be inspected the other day, did they ever find anything?"

"Yes, that is actually what I was going to talk about. When they were looking at it, they found that the brakes had been manually worn, or made to break on their own."

"So he cut the brakes?"

"No, not entirely. He used a saw or sander to wear them down enough so they would snap on their own if applied hard and fast, which is what happened. They believe Tyler Strange intended to crash the van, and wanted them to find the papers in his car and the letter to you."

"Wait," Alex turned back to Elijah, "there was a letter to me?"

"Oh, I thought you had heard. They found a draft of a letter that Tyler had written addressed to you. It was... Hostile to say the least."

"Can I read it?"

"Yeah, I brought it with me for you to read." Elijah took a piece of paper out of his briefcase and handed it to Alex. There were a number of markings around the actual writing, most of them drawings of Alex being shot.

> *Dear Alex Underwood,*
> *I promise, on my life and*
> *everything I stand for to kill*
> *you. You are like a virus, an*
> *insect that won't stop*
> *destroying lives. I will find*
> *you and the rest of your*
> *fucking family and kill you*
> *all. But first... First I will kill*
> *your grandparents. Blame the*
> *other grandparents for that.*
> *You should have taken the*
> *blame for hitting me*
> *Underwood.*

Alex read the letter and finished by throwing it on the ground. He walked over and sat on the couch, thinking about everything that had happened. If he had just accepted blame, nothing would have happened. A new trial, where he would have gotten maybe a few months in prison.

Instead, he let Andrew go to jail, his grandparents died and Mr. Hinsdale is in prison.

"Alex, was it really you who hit him after that day in court? Was it you or Andrew?" Alex sat on the couch in silence, his head buried in his hands. "Okay, well I have places to be. We can discuss this later, Alex. I left my number on the counter in the kitchen, call if you need something."

"I won't." Alex said finally as Elijah left the house. Alex got up and threw the letter in the garbage before heading up to his bedroom. He took the stuff out of his suitcase and made himself at home. Although it was still bigger than his old room and most for kids his age, his new room was fairly small for as big as the house was. He had a television, a king size bed, a couch and a closet.

Once Alex got settled, he got up to look out the window. There was a small forest on the backside of the house which separated the golf course and the house. He scanned the perimeter and yard with his eyes before he caught something moving amongst the trees. A person.

Alex went outside to see who it was, but found nobody. He searched the woods for almost an hour, but there was nobody out there, not even animals. He walked back inside, past his oblivious grandparents. When he got back to his room, he was shocked by what he saw inside.

"Damn man, this place is insane!" Nathan said, turning the television on, "Is this where we are staying for now?"

"Why the hell are you here? How did you even get in here? And why do you keep saying 'we' around me?"

"Because you need me, Alex. Plus, I got no home, so I just follow you around. And I'm here for a very important reason; to help you hone your skills."

"What do you mean?"

"Well, you made progress by killing the Blackstones, it was impressive, I'll give you that much, but the execution was piss poor. You barely cleaned up, you left them for the undertakers to find, and you didn't even clean out their wallet!"

"I only did it because they deserved to die, I didn't need their money. Nobody deserves to die now, so how do you expect me to hone my skills with you if I don't need to kill anyone?"

"Well, nobody needs to die, but we all die eventually right? Some just happen to stumble into the wrong place at the wrong time and find it sooner than most."

"You are psychotic Nathan."

"You are damn right I am! I am because I can be. Because I am free, and it feels so good. Seriously, you should try it sometime."

"Okay, so hypothetically, who would it be you want to kill?"

"To be honest, I am not sure. There are plenty of good options. The new lawyer, Elijah, the grandparents, Andrew, his mom-"

"I am not killing them! His mother is amazing and he is my best friend. I can't kill Elijah either, it would be too suspicious."

"All right, so, grandparents it is." Nathan hopped up and started walking out of the room.

"No," Alex said, stopping him, "I may hate them, but I could never kill them. They are shitty grandparents, but they have never done anything to deserve death."

"Oh yeah?" Nathan said, walking out of Alex's room and into the grandparents, "Well how about this?" He opened Alex's grandmother's laptop to reveal a string of emails sent to Tyler Strange. Some asking him to win the case, some worse.

"They tried to buy the case," he said in shock, "they paid Tyler Strange to win the case and send me to prison. They wanted me gone so they could get everything my family left behind. When that didn't work, they threatened him into killing my other grandparents."

"So, gun, knife, or poison?" Nathan smirked.

"None. I have another way."

After several hours of preparing an elaborate plan to kill his grandparents with Nathan, Alex made him leave while he sat back and waited anxiously to watch it happen. The plan was simple: turn them on each other. Alex could tell they were only still together so they wouldn't have to split the money, so it should be easy causing a fight between the two.

"Hey Grandma, Grandpa, can I talk to you guys?" Alex called from the kitchen right before bed.

"What do you want Alex?" His grandmother said in irritation.

"I just wanted to let you know, Grandma, that I found out that your husband here has been putting money into a separate account each paycheck."

"How did you know that you little brat? That was a secret!" His grandpa yelled.

"How could you be doing that? That is our money! Both of ours!"

"Oh, hang on guys," Alex interjected, "I have a way to solve this. End all of your problems."

"How?" They both asked.

"Here. There is a gun in the top drawer by the sink. There are two bullets in it. I am going to go out for a while, and when I come back, you better both be dead. Okay?"

"And what if we don't want to die today? What if we throw the gun out? What if we turn you in to the police?"

"Then I come back and kill you myself." Alex said and he took the car keys and walked out. He drove off and called Mr. Crow to see where he was.

"Hello?"

"Hey Mr. Crow, it's Alex. Could you meet for coffee or something?"

"Yeah sure, how about the Starbucks down by the Old Navy?"

"No problem, see you there."

When Alex got there, Mr. Crow had been waiting. Alex sat down with him and started talking.

"Do you know when Mr. Hinsdale will be getting out?"

"No I don't, when we were there I was taken away almost immediately, so I had no time to talk to anyone really. I think there will be a trial though."

"I wouldn't be surprised; he is in a lot of trouble. How are you doing though Alex? You seem…different lately."

"I am fine; I don't feel any different." The two continued making small talk for a few minutes before parting ways. Alex went back to his grandparents' house to see if they did it. He walked into the kitchen to the smell of gunpowder and saw both of them lifeless on the floor. He smiled and took out his phone.

"911, what's your emergency?" The operator said upon picking up the call.

"Hello, operator. My name is Alex Underwood, and I would like to report a death."

"What kind of death?"

"I was at my grandparents' house and they were arguing and to escape it I left to go have coffee with one of my old teachers and when I came back they were both dead by gunshot, it looks like a murder-suicide."

"All right son, what is the address?"

"4572 Redbird lane."

"We have officers en route now, just stay there and they will take care of it."

"Thank you so much." Alex hung up and started laughing hysterically. His plan had worked like a charm. It was too easy.

He waited about 20 minutes before the officers arrived. One of them, Officer Pierce, went to talk to Alex.

"All right, Alex, what the hell happened here?"

"My grandparents were fighting, and while I was gone, killed each other."

"Okay, well we are going to go check it out. I will have an officer out here to keep an eye on you."

"No problem, thanks for coming officer." Alex walked around to the side of the house when his phone started ringing. It was Hailey, his old girlfriend.

"Hello? Hailey, what is-"

"Alex! You have to help me please!" Hailey cried into the phone.

"Hailey, what is going on? Are you okay?"

"No I'm not, he is going crazy. Please come help!"

"Okay, okay, well where are you?"

"I'm at-" She tried to get the words out, but then she went silent.

"Hailey? Hailey!" Alex screamed into the phone. All of a sudden he could hear her screaming on the phone. He could hear her shouting, along with muffled sounds of punches landing. She was being raped. Alex stood with his phone to his ear as she was being raped on the other line. The screaming and moaning suddenly stopped.

"Don't come looking for her." A voice said on the other end before hanging up. Alex crushed his phone with his hand before throwing it on the ground and running to his grandparent's car. It was Carter. He knew it. Alex sped off in the car in search for Carter and Hailey. Nathan stood on the side of the road and smiled as Alex passed. His plan was coming together.

Chapter 13: Seeing Red

Alex drove with a purpose back into town. He didn't know exactly where he was going, but he knew wherever it was, he had to get there fast. He finally decided to go to Hailey's house first to see if her parents knew where she was.

Luckily, Alex knew right where her house was. After dating for a few years, he had been to her house plenty of times. It was on the opposite side of town though, and Alex couldn't help but think he was driving right past wherever she was the whole time. When Alex got to her house, her mother was already on the porch.

"Alex, what are you doing here?" She asked.

"Mrs. Nelson I need to know where Hailey is and fast, I think she may be in danger right now and I need to make sure she is okay."

"You and me both. I have been trying to contact her for an hour and she just is not picking up."

"Where did she go tonight? Who was she with?"

"She went on a date with Carter tonight. They went to dinner at the Olive Garden and then to his house for a movie."

"Where does he live?"

"Alex are you okay? I know you are upset about breaking up, and you probably don't like her dating someone else so soon after the two of you split up, but Carter is a good kid."

"Mrs. Nelson, please don't freak out, but I have reason to believe Hailey was raped tonight and I need to find her." She stood on the porch in shock and broke into tears.

"No, no, please not my baby, not her," she begged.

"I am so sorry Mrs. Nelson, but that is why I need to know where he lives. I think it was him and I need to be sure."

"I have no idea Alex; I am so sorry. Try going to Olive Garden and asking them if they talked about going anyplace else. Just please bring my baby back, Alex."

"I promise I will make sure she is safe." Alex got back in the car and left for Olive Garden, thinking about what Nathan would do. How much easier it would be if Nathan was with him.

Alex pulled into the Olive Garden parking lot and hopped out of the car. He ran inside and saw a waitress at the register with nobody else around.

"Excuse me, waitress," Alex approached the desk, "did you happen to see a young couple come in tonight?"

"I am sorry sir, a lot of young couples come in here every night, you will have to be a little more specific."

"The girl about 5'4", the guy about 5'6" or maybe even 5'7", I don't know, but the girl's name is Hailey Nelson, the guy's name is Carter Branch."

"Yes, I do believe I remember a couple that fit that description. Why are you asking us if they were here?"

"Because I think she is in trouble with him and I need to find them before he hurts her even more than he already has."

"Well I wish I could help, but after they ate they got in his car and went south, that's all I know."

"What kind of car?"

"A blue Toyota car if I remember right, a four door."

"Thank you, that helps."

"I hope you find her okay son; I can tell she means a lot to you. The one who got away, right?"

"Yeah, I guess. More like the one I lost."

Alex left the Olive Garden and drove south. Down in South Wendle was mostly housing developments. Most of the kids at Alex's school lived down there, so that was his best chance at finding Hailey.

He drove down through three neighborhoods with no luck whatsoever. After a half hour of driving blind, he thought about quitting. He sat in his car on the side of the road in one neighborhood and started punch the steering wheel. Out of nowhere, he heard a voice.

"Damn man, you seem a little angry." Alex looked out the window to see Nathan. "I like it."

"How are you here again? How do you always find me?"

"Oh Alex, you just don't understand how much time I have on my hands do you?" Nathan laughed, "Now look, you can't give up yet. This is the perfect opportunity for you to get a sixth kill! Six!"

"I had planned on it, yeah."

"Well, have you thought about *how* you were going to do it? Hide it?" Alex hadn't. The whole time he had been so angry, he never stopped to think about how he would do it if he found them.

"I don't know, I will probably just cut his throat and bury his body."

"And how did that work out last time? You see, this is why you need me Alex. I mean, without me you probably would have tried to kill your grandparents by making their ceiling collapse or something stupid like that."

"Fine, what do you suggest Nathan?"

"Well, I think we should torture him. Torture is a great tool to use when someone bad is not cooperating."

"Torture? We want to kill him, not torture him!"

"Fine, but it would be fun. I think the best plan is to cut him up into seven little Carter nuggets and hide each piece in a different part of the city."

"You know that is actually not a bad idea. But we still have to find him before we can use it. Do you have any idea where to find him?"

"Well, truth be told the best I got is keep looking at every house here in South Wendle and find the car. Find the car, find Carter."

Alex and Nathan drove around for about another hour together. Hope was quickly fading as they entered the final neighborhood. Five houses in, however, they found the blue Toyota.

He pulled the car up to the curb about two blocks from the house the Toyota was parked at.

"All right champ, what is the play here?" Nathan asked, turning to Alex.

"It doesn't look like his parents are home, so you take back I take front. We go in at the same time and find them. If you find Carter first, bring him to me."

"Go team go, let's do this. Here, take this gun, you will need it." Nathan handed Alex one of his guns with a suppressor on it. Alex nodded and the two got out and crept down the street to the house.

Alex stood at the front door and heard laughter from the inside. It all sounded like about four guys, no girls. He waited a few seconds, then he burst in through the door. He could see Carter among the other three guys, so he shot him in the leg as Nathan shot the other three in the head, killing them.

"You didn't have to do that; they did not deserve to die."

"Guilt by association, they deserved it." Nathan started dragging the three corpses outside while Alex watched as Carter lay screaming in pain on the ground. Alex shot him again, this time in the arm. Tired of watching it, he threw the gun across the room and started attacking Carter. Landed blow after blow, punch after punch on Carter's face. The screams slowly faded to moans, and then silence as Alex continued hammering away on him. His fists now completely covered in blood and Carter unrecognizable.

"Think he's had enough?" Nathan said from the corner.

"No," Alex said as he continued the assault on Carter. After a few more shots, he got up and cleaned off his hands, "Let's go find Hailey, she has got to be in here somewhere." Alex went upstairs and found nothing. When he opened the bathroom door, a fifth guy jumped out and attacked him. Alex managed to hold his own before Nathan came up and shot him in the stomach.

"Where is Hailey?" Alex said as the guy started coughing up blood, "Where is she?"

"Basement, basement." He managed to get the two words out before Nathan shot him in the head.

Alex ran down to the basement to find Hailey. He found her naked and face down on a mattress, her arms and legs tied to the bedposts Fifty Shades of Grey style. She was passed out at this point. She had bruises all over her body and Alex could see blood on the mattress. He untied her and brought her upstairs.

"Hailey," he said, walking slowly with her, feeling tears fall down his face as she started to wake up, "hey it's me, Alex. I am here for you." Alex hugged her close to him.

"Thank you Alex, these men are animals. The things they did to me…" Hailey tried to talk while sobbing into his shoulder. Alex held her tighter than he had held anyone before to show her she was safe with him.

"Don't worry, I got you. You're safe." Alex covered her with a blanket to soothe her. Nathan stood in the corner watching the whole thing.

"Well aren't you two just precious. What do you want to do next?"

"I am taking her home, you clean up the bodies and the house."

"Sounds good champ." Nathan went upstairs to get the other body.

"Alex, who are you talking to?" Hailey said, lifting her head off of his shoulder.

"It's nobody, don't worry. Come on, let's go home." Alex took her back to his car and together they drove back to her house. Her mother was waiting on the porch again when they got there, and ran off to them when Alex took Hailey out of the car.

"Thank you, Alex. Thank you so much. What happened?"

"I am not entirely sure; she will be able to tell you more when she is not in this state. From the looks of things, Carter and his friends raped her in his basement."

"Did you call the cops?"

"I wouldn't worry too much, Carter regrets it, I made sure."

"Okay, well don't tell me anymore, I don't need to know. Thanks again Alex, we will be in touch."

"Sounds good. Good night Mrs. Nelson." Alex went back to his car and watched her take Hailey inside. His heart broke a little as she disappeared into the house in her mother's arms. She too, was now like him. A little broken inside.

Alex sat in his car and wondered where he could go from here. He had no family left, his ex-girlfriend had just been raped, and his friend was in the hospital. He finally decided to call the only person left who wanted to listen to his problems; the only one.

Chapter 14: Demons

"Alex?" Mr. Crow said, answering the call, "It's almost midnight, what's up? Are you all right?"

"Yeah, I just needed to talk to someone. I'm sorry if it's too late."

"No, no it's fine. Do you want to come over? It may be a little easier that way."

"Yeah sure, I will be right over."

Alex drove off into the night to Mr. Crow's house. In the beginning, being with Mr. Crow was the only place he could be himself. Now, it's turning into the only place he can be at all.

At this time of night, the roads were lonely. He saw another car maybe every couple of miles or so. It was quiet, and he liked it like that. It allowed him time to think. He knew that in the next week he would go visit Mr. Hinsdale in prison and Andrew in the hospital.

When Alex pulled into Mr. Crow's driveway, the porch light came on and the door opened. Mr. Crow had a very nice house, or at least nice for a high school level teacher.

"Hey Alex, come on in." Mr. Crow said from the door. Alex shut his car off and made his way inside. He had never been to Mr. Crow's house, he liked it.

The inside of the house was just as nice as the outside. He had hardwood floors throughout the house, with shag carpets in some areas. He had a stone fireplace in the corner which Alex could feel the second he walked inside. The furniture was all black leather, and the bookshelves around the room filled with some of the greatest authors to ever put pen to paper.

"Wow, you have really done well as a teacher huh?" Alex said, sending his eyes on a visual tour.

"No, not really," Mr. Crow responded with a laugh, "I just make do with what I am given. Are you planning on staying the night?"

"Could I? I really don't have any other place to go."

"Absolutely Alex, I wouldn't force you out on the street on your own. Please, have a seat. Do you need anything to drink?"

"Yeah I will have a water." Mr. Crow went into the kitchen to get Alex some water.

"So Alex," he called from the kitchen, "you had a pretty bad couple of days huh?"

"Yeah, you don't know the half of it."

"Well we have all night, let's recap."

"All right, well Andrew got put in the hospital, so that was a fun start. I spent basically the rest of the day trying to get a job, that didn't work out too well. Then Mr. Hinsdale gets arrested for killing the Blackstones, so yesterday basically sucked."

"Was today any better?"

"No. Worse, honestly."

"What happened?"

"Well, as I told you when we got coffee, I was sent to be with my other grandparents for a while, and I left for a little bit because they were fighting."

"Yeah I remember. Did they settle their issues?"

"Not at all. When I had gotten back, they were both dead. Murder suicide."

"Oh my God, Alex..."

"It's okay, don't worry, I have learned to accept it. Death happens to all of us, I guess people I get close to just get it sooner than others."

"None of this is on you, Alex. You have to know that."

"Yes it is, of course it is. You know what else is on me? Hailey."

"What do you mean? Hailey Nelson? Your ex-girlfriend?"

"Yeah, that's the one. She was raped tonight. Carter and his friends."

"Did you report it to the police?"

"No, they wouldn't do anything. I went to his house and saved her."

"You didn't hurt the guys at all, did you?" Alex thought for a second before answering.

"No, of course not. They were out of the house when I got there, maybe they went to the store or something. Either way, Hailey is safe."

"That's good Alex," the two sat quietly for a few seconds.

"Mr. Crow, can I ask you a question?" Alex broke the silence.

"Sure, what is it?"

"Why do you stick around?"

"What do you mean stick around? In Wendle?"

"No, stick around me. Everyone else has either died or abandoned me, why do you stick around and continue to support me?"

"I know I don't talk about it much, but I understand you. When I was a kid, my father liked to drink. He would get drunk at a bar or at home, then come and get rough with my mother. If I tried to step in between them, he would hit me. A lot."

"Wow, I am sorry Mr. Crow, I didn't know."

"Don't be, nobody really does. One day, I got a letter from a rehab place. The counselor my mom was seeing about it advised them to get in touch. They said they could come and get my father and bring him there, all my mother and I had to do was say yes. I said no."

"Why would you say no? They could have helped him not drink so much, you guys could have been in a better place."

"I am not sure why I said no. But I did either way. That night, my sister was taking out the trash. She was a couple years younger than me at the time, 16. I was your age. My father decided to drive home from the bar that night. He drove too fast into the driveway and hit her. My father killed my sister because I was stupid enough to think he could change. So yeah, I understand everything you go through because I lost someone based on a decision I made too."

"Thank you for sticking around, Mr. Crow. Thank you for everything you do for me. Knowing that you went through that and it made you to be the person you are now proves I still have a chance."

"You have as good of a chance as anyone Alex. All right, well I am tired, let me fix up the bed in the guest room for you."

Mr. Crow left to make a bed for Alex, leaving Alex to his thoughts. He was going to see Andrew the next day, whether Andrew would be awake or not. Still, it would be another three weeks before Andrew could leave the hospital.

After the bed had been set, the two both went to sleep. Alex had started noticing a few things about his recurring nightmares; they were getting increasingly violent, and now Nathan was in all of them. Even the non-recurring nightmares had him in them. Alex couldn't figure out why, but he just couldn't get away from Nathan.

In one of the newer, more prominent nightmares, Alex was running away from a giant Nathan, who was trying to put Alex in a cage. Nathan would scream things like "you're mine", "I will put you in the cage you put me in" and "it's too late to run". It made him nervous to see Nathan, though Alex knew they were only dreams.

At around 7 A.M., Alex woke up to get ready to see Andrew. Mr. Crow was leaving around the same time, but he had to go to work at the school. Alex grabbed everything he needed and left for the hospital around 7:30.

When he got to the nearest hospital, he checked in at the desk. The lady was the same one from when his dad was at the hospital before he died, so she recognized him immediately.

"Welcome back Alex, I wish I could say it's good to see you here. Who are you trying to see today honey?" The lady said, handing him a visitors pass.

"Andrew Streeter, he was in a car accident. What room is he in?"

"Oh you are lucky, they just got him in late last night from Seattle. He is in room 58, down the hall to the right there. Hope he's doing all right."

Alex walked back to Andrew's room. It was a surreal feeling when he walked in, because the room looked identical to the room his father had. Andrew looked asleep on the bed, so Alex pulled up a chair next to the bed. He knew Andrew wouldn't hear him or respond, but he started talking anyway.

"Hope you are doing all right buddy. I am so sorry this happened, it was my fault, I should never have left the camp that morning. But there is something I need to tell you really quick, before anyone comes in. Carter raped Hailey, Andrew. I heard it all over the phone. Me and a friend of mine, Nathan went to his house and saved her. We killed them. Nathan and I killed all of them, Andrew, everyone. Carter and all his friends. It is okay though, like Nathan says, they deserved it. I hope you get out of here soon man, I miss you." Alex stopped talking when Mrs. Streeter came in the room.

"Oh, Alex, I didn't know you were here."

"Yeah sorry, Mrs. Streeter, I forgot to let you know I was coming by."

"Have you found a place to stay? I heard about your grandparents. I'm sorry."

"I am going to be staying with Mr. Crow until Andrew comes out of here, then I will come back in with you guys; if you want me, that is."

"Of course we do, Alex. I would let you come back now if you wanted."

"No, you don't need me in your way with all you have on your plate. Hey, have you heard anything about Mr. Hinsdale yet?"

"Yes, he will be held in a private trial today where the judge will make his decision."

"Private? That is terrible, I wanted to be there."

"If I hear anything I will let you know, okay?"

"Thanks." Alex left the room and headed back down to his car to go home. He knew they would put Mr. Hinsdale away for life, the evidence was too much. It was hard to think about, but it was true.

Three weeks after that day, Alex went back to live with Andrew and his mom. Things had finally settled down for those few weeks, and it was nice. The only downside was Mr. Hinsdale being put in prison to await the death penalty for the murders. He was not allowed visitors either, so Alex couldn't see him.

Alex had gone to Andrew's house while his mom was on her way there with him. Alex hadn't been able to actually talk to Andrew since the accident, so this was a good day. When they arrived, Alex saw the wheelchair Andrew had to be in.

"Hey welcome home, man!" Alex said with enthusiasm, "How are you feeling?"

"Fine." Mrs. Streeter shut the door and left the room, leaving the two alone. "We need to talk, Alex." Alex and Andrew moved into the living room.

"Yeah definitely, it's been almost a month, a lot has gone down. Like Mr. Hinsdale, he-"

"Shut the hell up Alex, please. I don't want to hear it."

"Jesus, what is your problem?"

"You killed Carter and his friends, Alex."

"Wait, what do you mean?"

"Don't play stupid Alex, you told me in the hospital a few weeks back. You thought I was asleep but I wasn't. You admitted to killing them."

"If you listened to me at all then you knew they deserved it." Alex said back in a hushed tone.

"Nobody deserves death, nobody. I think you killed the Blackstones too. Jesus, you probably even killed your grandparents. What's next? Me? My mom?"

"You are my best friend; I would never do anything to hurt you or your mother! Why are you doing this?"

"Look, Alex. I want you gone, now. I still love you like a brother, and I don't want to see you like this. You are nearly at your breaking point and it's terrifying. My mom has called the cops and they are on their way here now, if you leave you have a few minutes to get a head start, but you have to leave now."

"You motherfucker," Alex said as he slowly walked towards the door in shock.

"Please leave Alex, for the safety of all of us, leave now."

"I trusted you! You were supposed to be my friend!" Alex screamed as he ran out the door.

Andrew had betrayed him. Years of friendship, thrown out because Alex got justice for Hailey. Alex was furious, but he knew he had no time to be mad. The police were coming and he needed to run. He ran towards the trees. About a quarter mile in, he heard Nathan call out to him from a small shack.

"Hey Alex, over here!" He called. Alex ran to the shack and got inside. "Where do you think you are going there hot rod?"

"Andrew betrayed me, he called the cops."

"Well you will be safe here, welcome to my humble abode."

"I thought you said you were homeless?"

"I am, but I stay here most nights. It's abandoned and nobody ever comes around unless they are running from the cops, which only happens every couple of weeks."

"So what are we supposed to do? Hide here our whole lives?"

"No way, live like I do. You will do everything I do, it'll be fun, like we are one person."

"Well obviously living on the street has worked out for you so far, so let's try it."

"Now that's the spirit! Come on, we have a lot to do." Nathan and Alex got up and left the shack to go cause trouble. Alex was on the run from the cops now, and it was time to let Nathan take the wheel for a little while.

Chapter 15: Nathan

Alex and Nathan each grabbed a gun and a water bottle and set out to the town. Alex was intrigued to see how Nathan lived. It seemed to him that Nathan would just randomly show up when it was convenient. Living in Nathan's shoes for a while would serve Alex well, showing him a new side of things.

"So what's the plan?" Alex said as they walked through the trees, "We have to avoid the cops no matter what."

"Yeah I know; I am thinking we should rob a gas station. Maybe kill a few homeless bums while we are at it."

"Wow, you really are crazy aren't you?"

"Not crazy, Alex, creative. I look at myself as an artist. An artist who needs to express himself in order to be truly appreciated."

"Artist? What do you do, paint the streets with blood?"

"Absolutely. You know, one of the things I plan to teach you while we are out here is appreciation."

"What kind of appreciation? I appreciate a lot of things as it is, what more could you teach me?"

"No, no, no Alex you appreciate what you have been given in life: Food, money, happiness, life. I am going to teach you to appreciate what you *take* from others:

Food, money, happiness, life. Only then will you know how great it is being me."

The two continued on as lone wolves on the path to oblivion, all the way into the other side of town. They agreed that the first thing they should go do was to get Alex a new outfit. Andrew would have no doubt told the police what he was wearing, so it was smart to get a quick change of clothes. Luckily, there was a Goodwill store nearby.

"Is it really smart to be stealing from Goodwill?" Alex asked as they approached the store, "I mean the place is just what it claims to be, a place of good will. They have low prices so people like us can buy them."

"No, they have low prices so people like you could buy them. They have shitty security so people like me could steal them. Now, since you are me, we can steal them together."

"I don't know man; I just feel like this will bring on some wicked karma."

"Ah I don't believe in all that garbage. If it was true, I would be up to my neck in shit by now but hey, these hands are cleaner than a baby's asscrack."

"You know Nathan; I think a baby's asscrack wouldn't be very clean at all." Alex replied with a laugh.

"Don't test me boy, I like you, but I'll still kill you." They walked in the store and headed for the clothing department. Since it was almost winter, the majority of the department was winter goods. Gloves, hats, heavy jackets and snow attire like boots and pants. There was a small section just past it that had the clothes Alex intended on getting.

A few workers had noticed the guys checking out the clothes and thought they were a little suspicious, so they sent the manager over to watch them. Nathan noticed it quickly and came up with a fast plan.

"Oh shit, manager coming. Stall him and go along with whatever I do; say you have a question about something." Nathan stuffed a shirt into his pants and straightened himself up.

"Doing all right over here?" The manager inquired.

"Absolutely sir, finding things just fine. Could you direct me to the bathroom though? I have diabetes and need to check my blood sugar, I am feeling a little lightheaded."

"Over here, son." The manager took Nathan over to the area where the bathroom was. He stood outside as Nathan went in, making sure nothing was going on. Before Alex could do anything, he heard an alarm go off.

"Fire! Everybody out!" One of the employees yelled from the front of the store. The manager ran off to help people out and Nathan came out of the bathroom.

"Nathan what did you do?" Alex said as they ran to the clothing department.

"Held a lighter near the smoke detector, sure way to get out of this. Grab what you need and let's get the hell out of here."

They grabbed some essentials and ran for the door, blending in with the rest of the crowd to make it out freely. Alex changed in a nearby bathroom. Alex dumped his old clothes in the garbage of the restroom and came out.

"So, where to next?" Alex said, emerging from the restroom.

"I am thinking I want an easy dinner tonight. What are you thinking?"

"I think hot dogs sound amazing right now. What about you?"

"I think you are right. There is a gas station down this road here, I hit it all the time, it's an easy take for us. Run by an old Asian dude. Super liberal, doesn't have a gun behind the counter."

"What kind of moron owns a company and doesn't keep a gun behind the counter for people like us?"

"This moron. We can take some fire starter and beer, too. Have ourselves a little cookout tonight."

"Hey, sounds good to me. I love camping."

As they approached the gas station, Nathan took out the gun and made sure it was ready just in case. He was sure it would be easy pickings, but things can always go wrong. The man in the shop saw them walking and moved everyone to the back of the store.

"What are you doing here? Why do you have a gun?" The man said nervously.

"We need hot dogs, fire starter and beer and we will be out of your hair. Alex, go grab the beer."

"Alex, who's-"

"Alex is a friend of mine; I'm showing him the ropes. Pretty soon there will be two of us running around all the time. We will own this town."

"Let's go we have everything." Alex said, tugging at Nathan.

"Yeah hang on." Nathan stepped forward and shot the man in the shoulder.

"What the hell was that for?"

"I feel bad for the guy; he is just a simple man owning a shop. Might as well give him some paid vacation time."

"Fine, let's go now."

Alex and Nathan ran out of the shop with the stuff and headed back towards the small cabin Nathan stays in. Alex loved doing this, it gave him a rush that he had never experienced before. It felt good. He was ready to spend the rest of his life doing this with Nathan.

When they got to the cabin, it was starting to get dark. Nathan started up a fire while Alex grabbed a few sticks to cook the hot dogs on. It was going to be cold that night, so although the fire could give away where they were, they were ready to risk it.

"Hey do you want one dog or two?" Alex said as he prepared the food.

"Give me two, I will probably only end up eating one, but I know if I take cook two up, I can save the other for a midnight snack."

"You would eat a cold, precooked hot dog in the middle of the night? That's absolutely disgusting."

"You should try it man I'm telling you, it's amazing."

"I am going to have to pass on that one, sorry." Alex and Nathan settled down in the dirt as the fire started to pick up.

"So, enjoy being a menace to society today?"

"Yeah I guess I did, it's fun to be on the run from the cops. It is really fun to do all this while having that thought in the back of your mind that you could get caught."

"Exactly how I feel, which is why I think you should let me take over full time."

"What do you mean take over full time?" Alex laughed as he tried to thoroughly cook his food, "I am letting you show me how things are done, isn't that the same thing?"

"Oh my God, you still haven't figured it out yet, have you?"

"Figured what out?"

"Damn, I knew you were stupid Alex, I didn't know you were that stupid. I really overestimated you."

"What the hell are you talking about?"

"Me, you, everything that's happened so far, it's all connected."

"How is it connected?"

"I am not real Alex." Nathan said as he bit into his hot dog.

"Yes you are, you are sitting right across from me."

"No, Alex. You just think I am. I am you, a vision you created to help you cope. It started after your dad died with the pissy attitude and occasional nightmare."

"That's impossible."

"No, it's not. Over time, after all the shit that happened, I grew bigger inside of you. With each traumatic event in your life, your dark side grew closer and closer to being who you are. You project that dark side out as me in order to try and reason with what you were doing. You killed the Blackstones, you killed your grandparents, you killed Carter and all of his friends, you even planted the knife in the car to frame Mr. Hinsdale. You have been seeing me more and more lately, right?"

"Yeah, I guess I have." Alex stared at Nathan with a confused and angry look.

"That's because you are getting closer to your breaking point. You are almost there now, in fact you are so close that until you hit it, I will always be here."

"And what happens when I do hit the breaking point?"

"You become me. I take over. There will be no more Alex, just Nathan. Once you finally break, you will never be able to come back."

"How do I stop myself from reaching that point? What can I do to prevent you taking over?"

"Death. That's the only way to go back. Whether it's by natural causes, murder, or suicide, the only way I don't take over is if you die."

"Why didn't I see this before..." Alex threw his stick in the fire and stood up.

"I think it's a disorder of some sort; but don't worry, all the cool kids have it. Basically, anytime you thought you were talking to me or about me, everyone else just thought you were crazy."

"I am crazy. Obviously I am because this whole time I thought you were real, that you were my friend."

"Well, we can figure this out later. You might want to run." Alex watched as Nathan faded away into nothing. He turned around and saw several officers with lights sprinting towards him. Alex started to run, but couldn't get away. One of the officers took him down and pinned him on the ground.

"Alex Underwood you are being placed under arrest for the murders of Carter Branch, Sean Finley, Aiden Small, and Will Finn." Alex started to hear white noise as the officer read him his rights and took him out of the forest and into the car. Alex had gotten himself stuck deep under a pile of his own shit, and now, he had to try and dig his way out. Perhaps the only way to do that would be with the help of Nathan.

Chapter 16: Locked Away

For the whole ride in the car with the cops, Alex was thinking about what Nathan had said. Was it true? Could he really just have gone crazy after everything had happened? It was entirely possible, but Alex couldn't believe it. Whether he was real or not though, Alex had gotten into a situation he couldn't get out of.

"So are we headed to prison or the county jail for now?" Alex asked the officers.

"Prison." They responded.

"So I don't get a trial? No chance to prove myself innocent?"

"We heard your confession on the surveillance video from your friend's hospital room. You will not receive an open trial, but instead a closed trial like your old lawyer Dave Hinsdale got."

"And how exactly does the court decide if it will be open or closed for everyone in custody?"

"If there is a confession, video or audio of it happening, or DNA evidence, it is closed. They do it that way because at that point, you are going to prison no matter what, it is just a matter of how long."

"How long do you think it'll be for me?"

"Well, your buddy Dave got life without parole and with the possibility of death row, pending further confession or evidence. He got that for two murders. You killed four guys, so I guarantee you will get the same, if not guaranteed death penalty."

"Well, we will have to wait and see." Alex sat in the back of the vehicle in silence the rest of the way to the prison. How could he prove that it wasn't him who fired the shots? It was Nathan, not him. And if Nathan was right, and he was just a projection of Alex's split personality, it still was just Alex not being himself.

When they arrived at the prison, Alex looked at everything a little bit differently. He had always looked at the fences and walls as necessary in order to keep the criminals and fiends inside. Now, as he prepared to be placed inside them as one of the criminals, they seemed rather annoying. The guards at the gate allowing the vehicle through looked meaner than they usually do. The car pulled up near a door and stopped.

"All right Underwood, out of the car." One of the officers opened the car door and pulled Alex out. "Follow us."

Alex followed the officers into the building and down a long, monotone hallway. Everything inside smelled like week old eggs and sun burnt piss water. They approached a window and saw a lady inside.

"Hey Carla," the officer greeted her, "new inmate today. I'd say he would be about a size 12, what about you?"

"I think you're right officer." The lady got up from her seat and disappeared into the back.

"In a few weeks you will get the white outfit, join gen pop. But until then, you are in protective custody in orange garb while you wait for your hearing."

"Awesome, prison orange is my favorite color," Alex said with a bit of sarcasm.

"I wouldn't be too cocky kid; this place is the real deal. It'll mess you up if you're not careful."

The lady returned with an orange-colored suit and handed it to the officer, who handed it to Alex. They continued through a few more doors and down another hall before seeing a few guards and a man in a suit, presumably the warden.

"Is this Alex Underwood?" The man in the suit asked.

"Yes sir, fresh out of the woods."

"Ah, thank you officers, we can handle him from here." The officers handed Alex over to the guards. "Welcome to Oregon State Penitentiary Mr. Underwood, my name is Warden Pinky. Now, we don't have too many strict rules outside of the normal here. Obviously you may not attempt to leave or touch the fences, and there is absolutely no tolerance for physicality or aggression towards other inmates or guards. Also, in regards to when I am in the room or on the intercom, when I talk you listen and when I ask a question you answer it correctly. Do you think you can survive under those rules?"

"I think I might just be able to manage, sir." Alex said.

"Good. Guards, put him through the wringer and bring him home." Warden Pinky walked away as the guards took out their batons.

"Strip down, place your hands on the wall and spread your legs, now." One guard ordered.

Alex did as he was told. One of the guards began inspecting his clothes while another went through the orange prison suit. All the while, Alex stood naked against the wall.

"You guys having a party back there or can I put my clothes back on?" he asked without turning around.

"Quiet Underwood!" One of the guards hit Alex in the back with the baton. "All right, second door on the right here, go in and make it fast." Alex walked down and looked in the room to see it was a bathroom.

"So what am I supposed to do?" He asked, afraid of the answer.

"Sit down and push out whatever you have stored up there. If you don't try or nothing comes out, we go in." The guards pushed Alex into the room and made sure the door stayed open behind him.

A few painfully awkward minutes later, Alex walked out of the bathroom and suited up in the orange outfit. Finally, it was time to go see his room.

"All right Underwood, this is your room until the hearing. It has an uncomfortable bed that you will sleep on, a dirty toilet to do your business in, and a sink that barely works. The window is too small to crawl out of with all your bones intact, by the way. Trust me, people try. Even if you make it out, you will have broken bones and you won't get away. Any escape attempts are shoot on sight for the tower guards. You don't leave until we say you do, and we bring meals to you. Enjoy your stay."

Alex sat down on the bed and got comfortable as the guards left, shutting the door behind them. The room wasn't so bad, just small. He got up and walked over to the window to see what was outside. The window was definitely small, about the size of a shoe box. Lucky for Alex, he had no intentions to try to escape.

"You really have been moving around a lot lately haven't you?" Nathan said on the bed.

"What are you doing here?" Alex asked, turning around to see him there.

"I just thought I would come and knock some sense into you."

"I don't need sense knocked into me, I am fine just like this."

"No, I don't think you are. Because while I was digging around inside your head, listening to your thoughts and everything, I could've swore I heard you don't plan on getting out of this hole."

"You heard right, I don't. I am fine right here. This way, you can't hurt anybody."

"We will talk about that Later buddy. Right now we are very tired, and we are going to sleep, right?"

"Yeah, sure." Nathan disappeared as Alex walked over and went to sleep. He didn't dream about Nathan chasing him that night. This time, Nathan had caught him, and was trying to lock him away in a cage. The same cage Nathan had been locked in for so many years.

Alex had fairly low energy days leading up to the hearing. He had stayed in his room for five straight days, and was definitely ready to move out. The guards had grabbed him in the morning and took him to the inmate waiting room to wait for the hearing. After six long hours, it was finally time to go inside.

"Hello once again, Mr. Underwood." Judge West said when Alex was escorted through the doors. "I have to say Alex, I am extremely disappointed in you. You were given a second chance a few months ago and here you are now after killing four young men. What do you have to say for yourself before I sentence you?"

"I got a call from a former girlfriend who was crying out in fear to me, and then I heard her get raped over the phone. I knew who it was, so me and a friend of mine, Nathan, found them and killed them for what they had done. We were right and she was in the basement. You can lock me up, sure. But I will walk into this prison with my sentence with a big ass smile on my face, Your Honor."

Judge West looked at Alex in shock for a few seconds before looking down and picking through papers on his desk. He found the papers he wanted, cleared his throat and began talking.

"Well then, Alex, I have come to a decision. For the murders of four young men you will be given 35 years in prison. Any bad behavior reported, including but not limited to inmate or guard altercations will result in an extension of your sentence, which will come in ten-year increments. You are also to be moved from protective custody to gen pop immediately following this trial. Good luck, Mr. Underwood, you are certainly going to need it."

Judge West dismissed Alex and the guards and brought in the next inmate for a hearing. Alex had fully expected what was basically a life sentence, but hearing it said aloud was not fun. He made his way back down the long hallway maze with the guards. This time, however, he wasn't headed for the bathroom or his protective custody home; he was headed into the jungle. Never in his life had he been as nervous as he was the moments before being escorted through the doors and into the cafeteria where the rest of the inmates were eating lunch.

"Grab a tray and get some food Underwood." One of the guards said as he pushed him in through the doors. Alex looked around at the dozens of inmates eating with their white outfits as he stood there at the door, half their size and dressed in bright orange, almost begging to be pounded into nothing like clay.

"Inmate, get a tray and eat, now!" Alex heard one of the guards yell. "Lunch is only 30 minutes long, so eat up!"

Alex walked through the crowd of prisoners to get a tray, seeing faces he had only seen before on the television. Everyone watched him as he got in line to get food, and laughed as other inmates bumped into him and pushed him around like a cat in a doghouse.

After getting food, the next struggle was to find a place to eat. There were a number of groups around the room, each taking up almost a full table. There was the Aryan Brotherhood at one table, members of an all Mexican gang at another, and quite a few other gangs taking up the rest of the room. Finally, he found a section of a table with just a few older guys at it.

"Hey, is this seat taken?" He asked one of them before sitting.

"The fuck do you care newbie?" The man responded with a snarl.

"I'm sorry man, I didn't mean to intrude I just-"

"No, we are just screwing around with you, please sit." He laughed as Alex sat down. "So, what are you in for?"

"Four accounts of first-degree murder."

"Damn...murder, huh? Four kills on your resume?"

"No, I've killed nine people, I have just gotten charged with four."

"Gerry, I like this kid," he said, patting Alex on the back, "I want to help him out. You got a lawyer son?"

"I did, once. I screwed it up though. Then I was given another lawyer and I am guessing he abandoned me because I haven't heard from him in a long time."

"Well I am going to send you to the lawyer, okay? He is a genius, just about runs this place. He will help you out. Just go to the commissary after lunch, he works there."

"Thanks a lot. By the way, what's your name?"

"Randall Woodfield, but you can call me Randy."

Alex ate with the guys during the lunch until the bell rang, sending them out. Alex managed to sneak off to the commissary to meet with the lawyer. He approached the window and didn't see anyone inside. He rang the bell, but nobody came.

"Hey, I'm uh, I'm here to see the lawyer." Alex called through the window.

"Well, well, well, looks like you found him." Mr. Hinsdale came walking out from a side door to greet Alex.

"I was wondering when I would run into you here." Alex said upon seeing him.

"I wish I could say the same thing to you but, truth be told, I knew you would be in here sooner or later. Still blaming your imaginary friend for putting me in here?"

"Look, I am really sorry about all that. Nathan got out of control and-"

"Don't bullshit me Alex. There is no Nathan, is there?" Alex sighed.

"I don't know. For so long I thought he was my friend who wanted to help me. A few days ago, right before I got arrested, he told me I projected my inner demons to make an image of him. Am I crazy?"

"Absolutely. Not because of the Nathan, that's just split personality disorder, it's very common. You are just crazy for not realizing it sooner."

"So really it was me doing everything I saw Nathan do? Frame you, kill people, everything? He was never there?"

"Never. It's always been you Alex."

"I don't remember doing any of that."

"And you won't. When Nathan is in control for the brief moments he is, you don't know what you are doing. Be careful though, pretty soon he will take over permanently. Then there is no coming back from there."

"Thanks, it's been good to see you. I should probably get back though; I am going to get in trouble."

"And we wouldn't want that, would we? Take care, Alex."

Alex and Mr. Hinsdale parted ways, with Alex going to his assigned bunk. He stayed there for the rest of the day, thinking about everything Mr. Hinsdale had said. That night, Alex couldn't sleep. Anytime he would get close, Nathan would wake him up. After a while, Alex gave in.

"Nathan what the hell do you want?" He asked in a quiet tone.

"We have to get out of here man, and fast!"

"Why? We are not breaking out, it won't work."

"Yes it will. At lunch I overheard some other inmates talking about some guy named Rocco who has a grenade. If that's true, we can use it to blow a hole in the northeast part of the fence and escape through the woods."

"What are the odds he actually has it?"

"Better than the odds of us getting out without it. We have to at least try, Alex."

"Okay fine, but we need to kill him to get it. In the morning I will find a knife or shank of some sort and we will get it then and get out."

"Man, I love when you work with me." Nathan disappeared into the night as Alex thought about their plan. It wasn't much of a plan, but it could work. Or he could die. Either way, Alex would be free.

Chapter 17: Breaking Point

When morning rolled around, Alex wasted no time finding a suitable weapon to kill Rocco with. Luckily for him, there were always fun tools to be found in the tiles of the showers. Once he had the shank, he had to find Rocco.

That proved to be a difficult task, however, as everyone he asked either didn't know how to find him or wouldn't say. After a few hours, he decided it was time to go to the one person he knew would know where to find him.

"Back for more, eh Alex?" Mr. Hinsdale said from behind the commissary window.

"I need this to be quick and quiet, okay? Who is Rocco? And how do I find him?"

"Alex, why do you need Rocco?" Mr. Hinsdale's face turned from a perky grin to a concerned frown.

"He has something I need."

"Is this Alex talking or Nathan?"

"Just tell me where the fuck he is Dave, and quick!" Mr. Hinsdale stared into Alex's eyes, realizing he didn't recognize him anymore.

"Alex, I don't what happened to you overnight, but I think it's over. I think you have finally broken."

"I don't need your condescending bullshit; I just need to know how to find Rocco."

"He is in the laundry room, that's his job. He will be there until lunch, so I'd hurry if I were you."

"See, that wasn't so hard, was it Dave?"

"Don't you ever say my name like you know me. You aren't Alex. Not anymore." Mr. Hinsdale shut the window to the commissary as Alex started walking towards the laundry room. Mr. Hinsdale was wrong; he was still Alex. He was still in control.

In the laundry room, Alex found Rocco. He was a bigger guy with enough battle scars to scare anyone, but not Alex.

"Rocco?" Alex said when he walked in.

"Who's asking?" One of Rocco's boys asked.

"Me." Alex cut his throat with the knife, killing him." Everyone but Rocco out. We need to have a talk.

"Who do you think you are boy?" Rocco demanded.

"I am Nath- Alex Underwood, and I am getting out of here."

"Jesus, you can't even remember your own name?"

"Shut up! Now I hear you have a certain explosive that could aid my escape. Is that information true?"

"Well, if it is, why would I give it to you? Maybe I want it to aid *my* escape. What do I get if I give it to you?"

"You get to walk out of here."

"Oh, so you are going to kill me here?"

"No, I didn't say you would get to live, I said you get to walk out of here. The key word in that is *walk*."

"Fine Underwood, you win." Rocco climbed on a table and grabbed the grenade from the light. "But I want out too. You and me escape together, then we go our separate ways. Deal?"

"Sounds good to me." They shook hands and Rocco handed Alex the grenade. Alex in turn drove the shank into his neck, killing him there. "You see Rocco, I would've let you live, but you got greedy. Thanks for this though."

Alex put the shank in Rocco's hand and the grenade in his own pocket. He made his way to the courtyard and joined in with a jogging group. They ran the perimeter each morning for exercise, so it wouldn't look suspicious. He noticed they were approaching the northeast wall, so he had to think fast.

Without hesitation, Alex took the grenade out, pulled the handle and placed it in the back pocket of the jogger in front of him. Alex slowed down enough to avoid the blast, but kept jogging. As they jogged along the fence line, the grenade went off, killing the nine joggers and putting a significant hole in the fence. Alex sprinted for it as he heard gunshots at him. He managed to make it out and into the trees without getting shot, but he didn't stop there. He ran as fast as he could as long as he could to get away.

After running for about three miles, he reached a small road. A car approached from the left, which Alex stopped by throwing a big rock through the windshield. He took the unconscious driver out of the car, exchanged clothes and sped off down the road. He was free.

"We did it man, holy shit," Nathan said in the passenger seat, "what's the plan now?"

"Get out of town, the cops will be looking for us."

"Are you kidding me? Goddamnit I thought I taught you better than that. We have unfinished business back in Wendle. We need to get our ass back there and make that business finished."

"It will do nothing but lessen our chances of getting away from the authorities, our best chance is to leave now and forget everything."

"Alex, let me put this in terms you will understand. Your best friend, the person you have stood by through thick and thin, betrayed you and got you arrested. You have never done him wrong, but now he thinks he can get away with turning you in to the cops?"

"I guess you may be right."

"No, I am right. We need to go back to Wendle and finish this."

Alex agreed with Nathan and set course for Wendle. After a few hours of driving, they had made it into the town. Alex wanted to make this fast so they could get out and back on the road again, all while avoiding cops.

The first place he went was Andrew's house. Andrew wasn't there unfortunately, but his mother was. Alex walked inside to find out where Andrew was.

"Dear God, Alex!" Mrs. Streeter dropped some dishes when she saw him. "What are you doing here? You are supposed to be in prison!"

"Yeah I know, and Andrew is supposed to be here, but he isn't. Why is that Mrs. Streeter? Where did he go exactly?"

"No I... I won't tell you." Alex crept closer to Mrs. Streeter as she backed into the sink.

"Come on now, I just want to know where my friend is. Can't you just tell me that? Where is my friend Mrs. Streeter?"

"Alex, please..." Alex got right up against Mrs. Streeter and grabbed a knife.

"Don't worry Mrs. Streeter, I will make it quick. He won't feel a thing. Just tell me where he is."

"Never." She swung a pan around from the counter and hit him on the head, knocking him to the ground. She ran for the door, but Alex got up and chased her. He threw the coffee pot down the hall and hit her in the head before she could leave, knocking her unconscious. He drug her to the bedroom and locked her in the closet.

Alex started walking out of the house when he heard the phone ringing. It was Andrew. He let it go to voicemail with the hope that he may get to hear where he was.

"Hey mom, so you didn't pick up, maybe you are already on your way. Well in case you aren't, the colleges are at the school now and the doors open in a few minutes. If I'm not outside when you get here I am in the school, so just come on in. See you soon." Alex knew where to go. He went and took $5,500 from the house and set off for Andrew.

Before he could go there however, he had to run back to his old house to pick up something important. Something he couldn't finish things without.

The house looked relatively the same as it did months ago when Alex was last inside. The blood was still stained on the carpet, as they had not tried to get it back out to sell again. Before he got what he needed, he went over and looked down at the blood and stood where he was when he killed Darren. That was when it all started. He went out to the garage and got one of his dad's old guns from the cabinet. I wasn't the same, but it was compact and dangerous, and that's all Alex needed.

He drove off for the school with the gun, ready to finally put an end to everything. Months of pain. Months of heartbreak, all leading up to this moment.

When Alex got to the school, he parked on the sidewalk and used Mrs. Streeter's phone to text Andrew to meet him at the common area of the school. Alex got out of the car and started walking when he realized he locked the keys in the car. He brushed it off and kept going. Once he got to the meeting place, he sat and waited for Andrew.

Because Andrew was in a wheelchair, it took a little while before he showed up. When he finally did arrive though, he was shocked to see Alex.

"Alex, what the hell?" He said, stopping the wheelchair immediately. "Where is my mother?"

"Don't worry Andrew, she is fine. She is back at your house, resting."

"You son of a bitch did you hurt her?" He screamed.

"No more than she hurt me," Alex rubbed the back of his head, "I am here to hurt you though."

"And how do you plan on doing that Alex?"

"I am going to shoot you in the head."

Andrew and Alex stared at one another from a distance. Both undoubtedly wondering how exactly their relationship had gone so bad as to get to this point.

"It's not too late Alex, you can still come back from this. I know you, the real you. This isn't you."

"You are right Andrew, this isn't me."

"I don't think you have hit your breaking point yet Alex."

"That's where you are wrong Andrew. You see, I've already past my breaking point... I have been past it for a while, I just hide it well. I am not as strong as I would like to seem. It eats away at me every day... The only thing that has kept me sane is the thought of a life away from here, away from all this. I know that can't happen now though."

Alex raised his gun to Andrew right as Mr. Crow came running in from the side of the school.

"Alex don't!" He called out, jumping in front of Andrew. "Don't do this Alex, you know you don't want to."

"Stop calling me Alex! Alex is dead. It's just Nathan here now."

"I don't believe you. I think you still have a chance, all you have to do is put down the gun and walk away Alex.

Just walk away. Either way, I won't let you kill Andrew. I can't let you, you will have to go through me, and I know you can't do that."

"Okay." Alex pulled the trigger, shooting Mr. Crow in the chest. Alex started walking towards him and shot Andrew's hand as he tried to get away in the wheelchair. Alex walked up and shot Mr. Crow in the head to kill him, then approached Andrew.

"You motherfucker. You really are gone. Goodbye Alex." Andrew said as a tear went down his cheek. Alex let one more shot out to Andrew's head as a single tear fell down from his eye.

"It's Nathan." Alex dropped the gun as he noticed a large crowd of people coming his way. It was over. Everyone was gone. Now it was time for him to disappear. To start a new life. To be Nathan.

Chapter 18: The End

Nathan took off towards the sidewalk where he parked the car. He smashed the window and got in the car. There was blood running down his arm from the glass, but he had no time to take care of it. Nathan managed to get the car started and drove off. He didn't know where he was going at the time, but he knew he couldn't stay where he was.

He decided it was best to start driving west towards the ocean. There would definitely be a search warrant out for him, so he knew that if it came down to it, he would go north to Canada. Nathan drove for hours with no music or talking, just contemplating and trying to figure out what had happened. Just 24 hours earlier, he was happy. Now, his only friends Andrew and Mr. Crow were dead at his hand, and his lawyer, who had stood behind him through all of the wrong Alex did, Mr. Hinsdale was facing the death penalty for a murder he committed.

Once Nathan reached Gresham, he stopped at a gas station. The news already had his face on it. He filled up the car and wondered what he could do. There was no place he could go to be safe. No people who would take him in. Nathan finally decided that heading north of the border to Canada was the only option. It was not a great plan, but it was a plan. He drove off his normal path and went north, into Washington. His plan was to go up to Cape Flattery and rent a boat to go across the Strait of Juan De Fuca. It wouldn't be easy, but dying free sounded better than living in prison. Or worse, dying in prison.

Nathan stopped at a small town called Packwood at the base of Mount Rainier. His car was dying and he knew he couldn't make it all the way across the state, so he decided to stay there for a few days and lay low. He had $5,000 left from the money he took from the Streeter house, so he used some to get a haircut first. The only way he wouldn't get caught is if nobody recognized him. He decided to spend some more on clothes next. Large, red flannel service jacket, boots and some Carhartt jeans. He could barely recognize himself now, so he knew he would probably be safe to approach someone for work. It would be easier to get a job now that he was not recognizable as a serial killer. He trusted his instincts and went to a local construction site first.

"Excuse me," Nathan called up to a worker on a ladder, "I really need a job and I'm willing to work my ass off if you let me."

"Oh yeah?" one of the workers shut the drill down and came off the ladder to talk to him, "Say kid, you ever use a power drill? What about a nail gun?"

"Yes for both."

"Jackhammer?"

"Once."

"Huh," the worker looked over to his boss, who he motioned to walk over, "talk to him. The kid says he needs a job, seems like he knows his stuff."

"Hey son my name is Randy, I'm the boss on site here."

"I'm Alex. I can use all of the machinery and tools here, I worked on a job with my dad before he passed."

"Oh, well I'm very sorry to hear that son. How old are you?"

"Eighteen. Will there be any background checks before I start if I get the job?" Alex had to ask, because he had no way of stopping them from finding out who he really was.

"It's ok son I don't think that'll be an issue. Have you ever worked an excavator?"

"A few times actually, with a little refresher on how to run it I think I am pretty solid."

"Well there you have it. Our last operator quit a few days back so we need a new one, looks like you got the job. You start tomorrow at 7, don't be late. Oh and hey kid, what is your name? Can't just call you kid every day."

"Thank you very much sir, I won't let you down." Nathan thought about it for a second, "And my name is Nathan, by the way. Nathan Barrett." Nathan and Randy shook hands and walked away. He knew he wouldn't have this job for a long time, but for the time being, it would work. The last thing he had to do was find a place to stay. He couldn't stay at a hotel or motel because all of them in the northwest region had photos of him, along with name, height and a number of other ways to identify him. He had changed his appearance, but it was still him in a lot of ways. He decided to rent a cabin a few miles out of town. The town and surrounding area was just loaded with them, so she found one pretty easy. It was small, cheap, and cold, but it was a place to stay.

The property owner could only allow a max stay time of one month, so that was his plan. stay and live this life for a month, or until he was found by the cops, then head north to Canada.

When he got to the cabin, he settled right in. Nathan threw his shoes off and turned on the television. The first thing he saw was the last thing he wanted to see; a news story on him.

"Alex Underwood has been confirmed as the killer of high school teacher Jason Crow and longtime friend Andrew Streeter. Police say he may still be at large, so if you happen to see him, you are warned to keep far away and contact the police immediately." Nathan watched as his picture was flashed on the television. Luckily for him, he didn't look much like that anymore. He was prepared to turn off the television, but then he saw something that pissed him off.

"Let's go to our reporter on the scene for more information. Sandy?"

"This is Sandy Briggs at the Oregon State Penitentiary where I am prepared to speak with the suspect's former attorney, Mr. Dave Hinsdale, who has been staying here for a few months after being found guilty of murdering the parents of Darren Blackstone. We are waiting for him to be brought out by the guards so we can discuss the recent incident involving his client." Nathan threw his drink across the room. The last time he had seen Mr. Hinsdale was when he visited him at the prison. He wanted him dead, but there was nothing he could do about it. Nathan looked up and saw his former lawyer walk on screen.

"Thank you for sitting down with me today Mr. Hinsdale, I'm sure talking about Alex Underwood isn't exactly the way you would like to be spending your day."

"Absolutely not Mrs. Briggs, I am more than happy to give all the information I can about Alex."

"Oh good, I'm glad to hear it. Well let's start with the initial murders. You, of course, were hired by him to defend him. Now that the relationship is over, can you give us your personal opinions on that incident?"

"Everything I did and said was accurate at the time. I did not and do not believe he killed his family. He did kill Darren, but not his parents. Everything that happened in those trials were genuine."

"And was that the end of Alex's reign of terror so to speak?"

"Hell no. Alex confessed to me in a when we were in the cell when they had found the evidence that he killed Darren Blackstone's parents in the cemetery. He planted the evidence in my car and ran, framing me for the murder. He returned a few days later to ensure I would be sent to prison."

"He admitted all that?" Sandy was becoming increasingly intrigued.

"Well, he told me that it was someone named Nathan who planted it, and not him."

"And you didn't believe him?"

"Of course not. I didn't believe him because Nathan *was* Alex. All of us have a dark side. The ones who go through traumatic events tend to show theirs more often. Alex went through so much trauma in such a short time, with his father, his mother, his sister and his grandparents all dying, that he lost control. We all have a breaking point where we lose control and our dark side takes the wheel. He finally reached his. He called it 'Nathan' because he didn't recognize that side of himself. Nathan took over a good kid's body and turned him into a murderer."

"Do you think Alex will ever be able to overcome this and be normal again?"

"He's too far gone. He first lost control when he killed the Blackstones, and by the time he killed his best friend and his teacher, he was too broken to fix."

"Alex is currently on the run from police, do you have any idea where he would go? Any hints that could help the police find him in any way?"

"No. He would be out of the state by now, the country if he's smart. He probably went north, he has always liked the Olympic National Park, I would check there first."

"Do you have anything to say to him if he is watching this?"

"Alex," Nathan's face turned red with anger as Mr. Hinsdale stared into the camera, "if you are watching, I need you to understand two things. The first is I'm sorry. I failed you by letting your dark side take over. I tried to keep you together, but I couldn't. The second is, you need to kill yourself. Get a gun, a rope, a bottle of pills, jump off a bridge, it doesn't matter how you do it." The visual feed was cut, but the audio was still playing. "If there is any of the real Alex Underwood left in there, you will know that they only way to be free of Nathan and to stop causing pain to others and yourself is for you to be dead. Please Alex. Kill yourself, now."

The broadcast finally ended and Nathan threw the remote at the screen. Death wasn't an option. For Alex maybe, but not for Nathan. He would kill anyone who got in his way of a new life.

Nathan lived comfortably for a few weeks. The government had called off the nationwide manhunt, but kept his name and face everywhere. Well, his old name and face at least. He now had shaggy, greasy hair and what his co-workers called a "man's beard". He bought some new clothes so he didn't have to wear flannel and boots every day. Nike shoes and a black/grey sweatshirt. Sadly, he had to move out of the cabin the next day. Time to go to Canada.

Nathan drove down to the jobsite to let them know he was moving on. Once he got into town, he noticed there were government agents and police everywhere. He parked his truck at coffee shop and walked through the trees the for the last half mile to the site. Once he got there, he saw his boss talking to an officer. He couldn't hear much, but he did hear one thing: there was a sighting of Alex in the town, so they had resumed the manhunt for the day.

Nathan knew he had to leave. He turned to run and tripped over a branch. The officer caught wind of it and decided that Nathan needed to be caught. Nathan ran from the police through the trees. Because he had a decent head start, he was able to get in his truck before they saw him. He drove off west out of town. They hadn't made his face or vehicle, and the roadblocks were mostly diminished in order to find him, so he got out with ease.

Nathan drove north for two hours before hearing a troubling radio news broadcast.

"Attention residents of Idaho, Oregon and Washington state. Alex Underwood has been spotted in Packwood, Washington and is on the run from the police. He is believed to be heading north to Canada or west to the coast in a blue and white 2001 Ford. He has shaggy brown hair, a beard and is wearing jeans, a black and grey

sweatshirt and a black beanie. If you see him, contact authorities immediately." Nathan turned off the radio. He didn't know what else he could do. He could see a cop about a mile behind him, so he sped off. He saw the lights go on and he knew the end was near. As he approached the old family campgrounds in Brinnon, he looked to his left and saw the road leading to Murhut Falls. Nathan felt something inside of him start to struggle, and he turned off onto the road.

The whole way up the dirt road Nathan could feel that something struggling, trying to get out. Finally, he reached the mouth of the trail to the falls. He slowed the truck to where he could safely get out before he places a rock on the pedal and watched as the truck went roaring off the cliff, down to a booming end that could likely be heard for miles. He ran to the falls as fast as he could. When he got there, he clenched his fists and looked up at the falls as if he were David and it was Goliath. He climbed down the hill just to see there were two teenagers there, probably a dating couple. Nathan approached them with a rock and killed them both, dumping their bodies into the river.

Without hesitation, Nathan scaled the cliff and found himself at the top of the falls once more. He looked around and wondered where he was, almost as if he wasn't in control the last 20 minutes. All of a sudden he heard something deep inside his head, like a thought that wasn't his. It was Alex.

"You are finished ruining my life." Alex said. He closed his eyes and pushed himself down the falls. Alex won. Nathan was gone; but it didn't come without a price. He felt the wind and mist weave in and out of his fingertips and hair as he fell down to the bottom, just like he always wanted; before he hit the rocks below and quickly faded to eternal darkness.

A few weeks after the death of Alex Underwood...

"Hey honey, what are you watching?" Mrs. Nelson asked as she entered the room.

"Just the news again," Hailey responded, "I am just trying to see if they have any more information on where Alex is."

"I'm sure they will find him sooner or later, there are not many places he could have gone where they wouldn't, really."

"I know, that's what I am afraid - oh wait, here's something,"

"Ladies and gentlemen we have breaking news on the Alex Underwood hunt," the news broadcaster said, *"authorities say they have found what they believe to be the remains of Alex Underwood in a river up in the Olympic National Park. At this time are not sure how much of the body, is identifiable, if any, but it was found within feet of the clothes Alex was last seen wearing, so they will take the body down to the lab for testing."*

Hailey shut the television off and looked undeniably upset by the news. Her mother went over and sat next to her, if for no other reason but to comfort her.

"I'm sorry dear," she said, "Alex probably committed suicide up in the woods to rid the world of whatever monster he had become over time. He did good, you should be proud."

"I know, I'm happy for him but... I guess I just had this weird fantasy that he would come back and run away with me and we could be happy."

"Oh you know I wish life were like that." Hailey laughed with her mom and got up from the couch.

Hailey walked into her room to go to bed, hopefully to forget everything. The night did not go the way she had hoped, though. She was having more nightmares. They had been getting more frequent as of late, and it was discomforting for her. That night, she had one that drove her to do something crazy. She saw the same figure in this dream. It had been following her in her dreams, though she couldn't quite make out the face or any physical features. For the first time tonight, it talked to her.

"Go to Murhut Falls, Hailey," the figure said in a soft, slithering voice, "you will find peace there."

So that's what she did. She got dressed immediately upon waking up and left a note for her parents on the table. She had never been to Murhut Falls, but she knew where it was. It was a long drive, especially at night, but she finally got there around 6 A.M.

Hailey ran through the trail towards the falls, hoping to see no strangers wandering there. Lucky for her, the whole area was dead. Peaceful. She looked around on the lookout area and found nothing. A crash brought her attention to the top of the bottom tier of the falls where a log was repeatedly banging up against a rock. She climbed down and proceeded to climb up the wall and went to the top of the falls. To her disappointment, she found nothing there either. Hailey sat down on the edge of the falls, not knowing that she was in the same location as her former love in his final moments.

"If you wanted to give me a sign, now would be a good time." She said, starting to cry. Looking around, she started wondering how she could have been so stupid as to drive all that way because of a dream. That thought went away when she felt a tap on her shoulder. She was too frightened to turn around. A familiar voice whispered into her ear.

"Come with me, let's go explore."

Acknowledgements

Before I get started with the official acknowledgements, I would first like to thank all family and friends I do not mention by name for your overwhelming support as I embarked on this journey to self-fulfillment. It was truly appreciated. Now, without further ado I would like to personally thank each one of these individuals for their contributions:

Karla Rogers, Mother: Thank you for the undying support and helpful tips you provided me with throughout. It was the thing that kept me going through every bump and curve, and I could not be more grateful.

Kevon Ellis, Uncle: Thank you for the financial contributions you made in order to help make this possible. It was a huge help and I will forever be in your debt.

Andrew Black, Cousin: Thank you for being the photographer and cover designer/editor for me. That was one area I was clueless in and you are the best person I could think of to help. You did an outstanding job.

John Davis, Teacher: Thank you for being the most impactful inspiration to my writing to date. You changed the course of my life, and I am extremely grateful for that.

Eric Nieland, Teacher: Thank you for constantly pushing me to be better and forcing me to always rethink things before I finish. What you have taught me will stick forever.

English Teachers, Various: Thank you to *Peggy Dunbar*, *Jack Simonson*, *Debbie Dyer*, *Kristine French* and *Amy Sutton*. As my English teachers throughout my life, you each had a part in helping me reach my potential and pushing me to do great things.

Character Influences, Anonymous: Thank you to each individual in my life, be it family, friend, coworker or just another face who's personality inspired a character in this book. I will leave all names out to ensure privacy and security, as not all influences were positive, but know that I am very thankful to have an influence like you in my life.